He unlea

"Suchen," L

Nose down, Guthrie obediently searched the area, ranging farther and farther from the original scene, with Liam following. The park rangers and ISB agents watched Guthrie's progress, their tension palpable.

Liam watched Guthrie's body language, and when his partner looked up at him, he gave a nod of assent. Guthrie slowly made his way another twenty-five feet, then fifty away from the road.

If he hadn't been here, Isabella could have died. She could have—

A change in Guthrie's demeanor severed the thought. His partner circled a small area at the base of a rock formation...and sat.

Liam's heart dropped to his boots. This was worse than they'd thought. There was another victim.

* * *

DAKOTA K-9 UNIT

Chasing a Kidnapper by Laura Scott, April 2025
Deadly Badlands Pursuit by Sharee Stover, May 2025
Standing Watch by Terri Reed, June 2025
Cold Case Peril by Maggie K. Black, July 2025
Tracing Killer Evidence by Jodie Bailey, August 2025
Threat of Revenge by Jessica R. Patch, September 2025
Double Protection Duty by Sharon Dunn, October 2025
Final Showdown by Valerie Hansen, November 2025
Christmas K-9 Patrol by Lynette Eason and
Lenora Worth, December 2025

Jodie Bailey is a *New York Times*, *USA TODAY* and *Publishers Weekly* bestselling author who writes "soul-stirring suspense" filled with love, faith and intrigue. Her novel *Crossfire* was an RT Reviewers' Choice Best Book Award winner that was commended for addressing "the stigma associated with mental health services and the military." She is a mom and army wife who believes dark chocolate cures all ills. She lives in North Carolina with her husband and a Lab-husky mix.

Books by Jodie Bailey

Love Inspired Suspense

Trinity Investigative Team

Taken at Christmas
Protecting the Orphan

Pacific Northwest K-9 Unit

Olympic Mountain Pursuit

Mountain Country K-9 Unit

Montana Abduction Rescue

Dakota K-9 Unit

Tracing Killer Evidence

Captured at Christmas
Witness in Peril
Blown Cover
Deadly Vengeance
Undercover Colorado Conspiracy
Hidden in the Canyon

Visit the Author Profile page at LoveInspired.com for more titles.

TRACING KILLER EVIDENCE

JODIE BAILEY

If you purchased this book without a cover you should be aware that this book is stolen property. It was reported as "unsold and destroyed" to the publisher, and neither the author nor the publisher has received any payment for this "stripped book."

Special thanks and acknowledgment are given to Jodie Bailey for her contribution to the Dakota K-9 Unit miniseries.

ISBN-13: 978-1-335-95715-3

Tracing Killer Evidence

Copyright © 2025 by Harlequin Enterprises ULC

All rights reserved. No part of this book may be used or reproduced in any manner whatsoever without written permission.

Without limiting the author's and publisher's exclusive rights, any unauthorized use of this publication to train generative artificial intelligence (AI) technologies is expressly prohibited.

This is a work of fiction. Names, characters, places and incidents are either the product of the author's imagination or are used fictitiously. Any resemblance to actual persons, living or dead, businesses, companies, events or locales is entirely coincidental.

For questions and comments about the quality of this book, please contact us at CustomerService@Harlequin.com.

® is a trademark of Harlequin Enterprises ULC.

Love Inspired
22 Adelaide St. West, 41st Floor
Toronto, Ontario M5H 4E3, Canada
www.LoveInspired.com

Printed in Lithuania

And be ye kind one to another, tenderhearted, forgiving one another, even as God for Christ's sake hath forgiven you.
—*Ephesians* 4:32

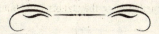

To Cathy...and God's beautiful story
of forgiveness and love

ONE

She wasn't usually known for following her gut into a bad idea, but...this might have been a bad idea.

Isabella Whitmore gripped the steering wheel of her small SUV, her knuckles white as she considered her next move.

The long gravel road stretched toward the horizon of the Badlands of South Dakota, seeming to go on forever. Deep crevices cut through the ground. Large rock formations hulked over the flatlands and cast eerie shadows across a landscape that made her imagine life on Mars. While she usually found the area beautiful, today she had to agree with John Steinbeck, who wrote that the area looked like "the work of an evil child."

It definitely felt evil now.

Somehow, the sun had slipped past early afternoon and was drifting rapidly toward evening.

She didn't want to be out here when darkness fell.

Although Steinbeck had also said that the Badlands became "lovely beyond thought" at night, none of that beauty mattered. Somewhere in this vast, otherworldly landscape, a kidnapper-turned-killer lurked.

And he was searching for women like her. Tall... Blonde... Alone.

Yep. This had been a very bad idea.

As the shadows lengthened, they seemed to hide a man with horrific intentions. The four women he'd abducted... How had they felt as he'd jammed a dark hood over their heads and dragged them away? What had they thought as they were abducted into the unknown?

The two women she'd interviewed today had said little about their actual attacks. As a forensic sketch artist, Isabella travelled this area frequently, and today she'd been in the border town of Meadowlark, North Dakota, interviewing the man's first two victims. She'd drawn the few details the women could remember.

Both women had been released within days of their abductions, dropped in the Badlands to fight for their survival. A third victim, Stephanie Parry, was still missing.

The fourth victim's remains had been found by hikers on the previous day. Calista Franklin's body had been sitting upright against a rock formation at the end of a gravel road in an area that occasionally attracted hikers and campers.

Clearly, the perpetrator was escalating. What would he—

A shrill ring tore through the car. Shrieking, Isabella jerked in her seat and gripped the wheel tighter. She forced herself to breathe.

It was only her cell phone. Shocking, since she was literally in the middle of nowhere.

Willing her heart to settle into place, she glanced at her car's screen. Caller ID flashed her roommate's name.

Isabella took a deep breath and pressed the button on her steering wheel to answer. Aiyana was not going to be happy. "Hey, Aiyana." She winced at her own fake cheerfulness.

"What do you think you're doing?" Pennington County, South Dakota Sheriff's Deputy Aiyana Macawi was always direct. Isabella had often accused her roommate of howling when she was upset. It was fitting that her surname meant *female coyote* in the Lakota language.

"I'm fine. There's no need to howl at me." Okay, maybe her nerves were less than fine, but physically, she was doing okay.

For the moment.

"Don't be cute. What are you doing roaming the Badlands in the exact area that some lunatic is dumping his prey? You know better." Like a lot of people, they had allowed one another to track their cell phones for safety reasons. Aiyana had definitely looked to see where Isabella was driving, and she was having none of the shenanigans.

Isabella searched for the road that turned off into an even more remote area, which the Park Service had set to off-limits to everyone but law enforcement. "I'm safe. I've got you watching my back."

"I'm two hours away. All I can do is watch helplessly if the little blip on my screen stops moving, or you go out of cell tower range and vanish." In her years on the sheriff's department, Aiyana had seen far too many crimes, particularly against Native American women. She was slightly paranoid, but that paranoia kept her safe. She was passionate about protecting women and was very aware of threats in the world. "Why are you there? The Badlands are nowhere near your route from Meadowlark back to Plains City. You're tempting trouble to find you."

There was no way she would tell Aiyana she'd been thinking the same thoughts. If her friend thought she was scared, she'd hop in her pickup to defend Isabella against all threats, real and imagined.

Still, she might as well be partially honest. "After talking to those two victims this afternoon in Meadowlark, I had to see where they'd been left by the kidnapper and where he left Calista Franklin. If I didn't make this drive, everything those women said today would rip holes in my sleep tonight."

Listening to them talk about their experiences as they'd processed and provided information had spun up horrible images about an area that was both beautiful and unsettling.

Aiyana was quiet for at least a mile. "I get it." She sometimes revisited crime scenes, trying to put the horrid images in her mind to rest. "But this guy's hunting, and he's after women like you."

"He's never kidnapped anyone out here. He's stalked and taken exclusively in Meadowlark. I'm not planning to stop at the crime scene, just to drive by."

Aiyana sighed. "What did the victims say? Anything you can share?" While the case was not in Pennington County's jurisdiction, Aiyana followed it with interest, like most local law enforcement officers.

"Not much. They saw nothing of his face, but they described him as being strong. The first victim saw his forearms. She said they were solid, muscular. She described serious burn scars on his hands and forearms. Victim two mentioned the scars and added that he had on a distinctive silver rope bracelet. I drew their descriptions, and Meadowlark PD is distributing them. We'll see if it helps." DNA evidence linked the victims to one perpetrator, but the man's DNA wasn't in any system that law enforcement could access.

"That bracelet could have meaning, although it's risky for him to wear something that could easily identify him."

"True. I can't figure out why he kept victims one and two for days and then released them, but he killed Calista Franklin and left her where she'd be found." It was certainly an escalation.

"Victim three, Stephanie Parry, is likely out there somewhere, waiting to be found. Given that he released one before he took two, and he released two before he took Stephanie... I hate to say it, but given the amount of time it's been since she disappeared, it's likely he killed her before he took Calista Franklin. He's out there now, hunting, and—"

"Thanks for playing mind games with me while I'm out here." Isabella shuddered. Sure, these was facts she already knew, but she didn't need them shoved in her face or her imagination. "The first two women reported feeling watched in the days before their abductions. I haven't felt anything like that, so let's assume I'm not on his radar." Although she did know how it felt to be watched, to be threatened...to lose everything because evil threatened the one you loved.

Evil from within her own family.

She let her gaze drift to the ring—his ring—that still glittered on her right hand. Things could have been so different if—

"Listen, Isabella, I don't like you wandering around in his killing field." Aiyana cut off her thoughts.

They were thoughts she shouldn't have been thinking anyway. "He doesn't have a *killing field*."

"But he left both surviving victims on a main road near you, and he left Calista Franklin's remains exactly where you're headed."

As if she didn't know. "You're not helping."

"Oh, so you admit you're nervous? That running around in the remote areas of—" The words fractured and the call dropped.

Isabella puffed out a frustrated breath as the Bluetooth disconnected and an '80s rock song filled the car. She glanced at the screen.

No more bars. She was officially out of touch with civilization, probably for the next fifteen minutes or so, when the next tower would pick her up.

Aiyana would be frantic, even though she knew how bad cell reception could be.

Isabella drew the corner of her lower lip into her mouth as she came to the turnoff she'd been searching for. A temporary barrier partially blocked the road, but she bypassed it. Technically, she was working with law enforcement, although that might not fly if she was stopped.

A mile or so ahead was the crime scene where Calista Franklin had been found.

Isabella had come to see if she could get insight into what the women might have seen, maybe even to pay her respects to Calista, but now that her cell wasn't in range and she hadn't passed another car in over fifteen minutes?

Bad idea.

She rested her index finger on the cross that hung on a chain around her neck, tucked beneath her shirt. It was yet another reminder of him, but it was also a reminder that she was safe in God's hands, even if she wasn't safe in the world.

Safe wasn't the exact word she'd choose right now.

Isabella checked her location on the downloaded GPS map. Only another quarter mile until—

A loud bang shook the SUV, and the steering wheel jerked. The vehicle swerved to the right and teetered, threatening to roll. Isabella gripped the steering wheel and turned with the skid.

The SUV rocked to a stop in a fog of gravel and dust.

Hanging onto the steering wheel as though it was the only thing anchoring her to the planet, Isabella gulped air so hard that her entire body rocked. When dizziness floated dark spots across her vision, she forced herself to breathe slowly before she hyperventilated into unconsciousness.

With a last whooshing exhale, she glanced around to make sure she was alone.

The SUV had stopped perpendicular to the road beside a tall rock formation.

No one else was in sight.

Dropping her head to the steering wheel, she breathed slowly until her brain cleared.

Time for a reality check. She was in the middle of nowhere with no way to contact civilization, and she'd probably blown a tire. The best thing to do was—

A thud rocked the car, and glass exploded from the driver's window. She screamed and whipped toward the door. Someone was there, but before she could register details, a blow struck her temple, and something dark descended over her head.

FBI Special Agent Liam Barringer tugged at the wrist of his black nitrile gloves, trying to get some air into them. The heat was brutal, but he needed to be here.

Calista Franklin's remains had been found sitting against a rock formation nearby, facing east, nine days after she'd been abducted from the small border town of Meadowlark, North Dakota.

A group of hikers had found her the previous day.

As much as he felt for the victim, he wasn't here to puzzle out her murder. He'd been assigned to something entirely different. The slight overlap of this case with the federal weapons smuggling investigation he was working had brought him into Badlands National Park in search of clues that might help to shut down a gun trafficking ring operating across North and South Dakota.

Liam booted a rock to the side. While he didn't expect to find anything, when it came to this crime ring, they could leave no stone unturned.

A loud bang and squealing tires tore through the air.

Liam looked at his SUV. It was undamaged, though his

K-9 partner Guthrie's head appeared in the rear window. The bloodhound had heard the sound as well.

Who could possibly be out here at this time of day, and what kind of trouble were they in?

Liam ran toward the sound. When he rounded a rock formation, he slowed to search the area. The Badlands were being their worst today, scorching the ground with the full force of summer. This was the kind of place that inspired sci-fi movies and nightmares. Some people thought the area was beautiful, but the towering rock formations scattered across the landscape looked like gigantic, oddly spaced gravestones. The canyons and crevices were like wounds.

About a tenth of a mile away, a small SUV idled perpendicular to the road. The passenger side front tire was blown, and someone stood near the open driver's door.

He stopped and winced. This was a bad place to break down. Not only could the heat and rough terrain pose dangers, there was now a ruthless serial kidnapper-turned-killer on the loose.

His visit to the park hadn't yielded new clues, but he could help this guy change a tire. He approached the SUV, his mind wandering to the case.

The kidnapper's initial victims had been locked away in darkness and assaulted for days before being released in the Badlands, bound and with black hoods over their heads.

Not so with Calista Franklin. Killing her then posing her remains with eyes open to the rising sun felt different. If DNA evidence hadn't linked the two kidnapped women and Franklin, Liam would have said that law enforcement was dealing with two different sick individuals.

He'd let his colleagues at the FBI explore that.

As a member of the Dakota Gun Task Force, a collaboration between federal, state and local law enforcement agencies, he was working with eight team members and their K-9 partners to expose and shut down dangerous weapons smugglers operating in North and South Dakota.

Evidence indicated that Calista Franklin had been dating a low-level runner in the ring. Brody Patterson had been arrested in a sweep a few weeks earlier. While he wasn't a key player, he had links to both Plains City, South Dakota and Fargo, North Dakota, where the ring was operating heavily. Law enforcement had been unable to link Brody to members of the Jones family, who appeared to be near the top of the ladder.

If Brody had ties to the traffickers, then Calista might have been linked to them as well.

Pulling off his gloves and stuffing them into his pocket, Liam continued toward the car. He'd give this guy a hand then head back to headquarters at Plains City PD. En route, he'd call the task force's supervisory officer, ATF Special Agent Daniel Slater, to—

A shriek shredded the silence, and the figure backed toward the SUV's hood.

Liam's adrenaline spiked, setting his feet into motion. Whatever was happening, that man wasn't the victim of a blown tire.

He wasn't a victim at all.

He was a predator hunting prey.

The man took another step back, struggling with a woman with a dark covering over her head.

She screamed again, and Liam reached for his gun. "Federal Agent! Stop and show me your hands!"

The man whipped toward Liam. He was tall, possibly over six feet, stocky and solid. He wore khaki-colored pants and a long-sleeved beige shirt that seemed to melt into the landscape. A dust-colored ski mask covered his face.

The man jerked his head toward the woman he was wrestling with, then shoved her away.

She hit the ground hard on her shoulder and cried out, then lay motionless.

Liam was almost there. "Federal Agent! Stop!"

The man ignored him and leaped into the driver's seat of the still-running SUV. He slammed the door and wrestled the car into an awkward U-turn, rattling away in a wobbly escape on the blown front tire.

He was getting away—the kidnapper the FBI had been hunting. Liam wouldn't make it back to his SUV in time to give chase.

Besides, his first priority was to help the victim. He closed the distance between himself and the woman, who was trying to sit up.

He looked from her to the SUV making its drunken way into the distance. He shoved his gun into its holster and bit his tongue to keep away words the old him would have used.

He couldn't pursue the attacker. His focus had to be the victim.

Liam slowed then stopped about five feet away. With a black ski mask pulled backward over her head, she wouldn't be able to see his approach. If he rushed up too fast, his footsteps would terrify her. "Ma'am? He's gone. I'm going to approach you and remove the mask."

The woman stilled, though her body remained tense as though she might flee.

Liam eased closer. "I'm beside you. I'm an FBI agent. My name is Liam Barringer. You're going to be—"

"Liam?" The woman struggled to sit up.

His name in her voice wrung inside his chest with a sharp, painful spasm.

He knelt beside her, refusing to believe she was who his

heart said she was. But her body size, the blond hair that straggled out from beneath the ski mask, the delicate fingers...

The sapphire-and-diamond ring on her right hand...

He nearly choked.

It was the same ring he'd placed on her *left* hand when he'd asked her to marry him four years earlier.

Closing his eyes, he took a deep breath to steel himself for the sight of her face, then gently took her hand and helped her to sit up.

"I'm going to take the mask off now." The words were so gravelly, she had to hear the tension and emotion.

Gently, he grasped both sides of the ski mask and eased it from her face.

Wide, terrified hazel eyes met his. That face, framed by wildly flying blond hair, was achingly, painfully, awfully familiar.

He was not prepared for the sight of Isabella Whitmore for the first time in three years, for the face he hadn't seen since the night before their wedding...when she'd disappeared. Now she'd turned up again in the middle of the Badlands. In the middle of this case...

The latest victim of a serial kidnapper.

TWO

Tremors shuddered through Isabella with such force that her teeth knocked together. She blinked rapidly, trying to free her eyelashes of hair strands that flicked at her eyes.

None of this was happening. It had to be a horrible nightmare. Maybe she'd hit her head. Maybe she'd fallen asleep at the wheel. Maybe she was at her apartment in bed, her mind the victim of a late-night nacho binge.

But no. Broken glass clinging to her clothes and a throbbing ache in her shoulder testified that she was very much awake.

And Liam Barringer's hazel eyes were mere inches from hers.

There was no way she'd been attacked and rescued by Liam. It was impossible.

Liam gingerly laid the knit mask aside and rocked back on his heels. His hand drifted toward her face, but then he rested it on his bent knee. "Did he hurt you? You landed hard on your shoulder." His gaze was sympathetic but guarded, and anger lurked behind it.

Was it anger at what she'd done to him, or anger at the man who had attacked her?

The man who had attacked her...

Everything rushed in like an avalanche. The car swerving... breaking glass...darkness...

She gulped against a spasm in her throat, but the sobs burst out. Gripping the front of Liam's gray button-down, she buried her forehead in his chest, humiliated to fall apart in front of him but too weak to hold herself up.

Everything spun in a chaos of confusion.

He stiffened, but then his arms went around her. While he didn't exactly pull her closer, he did keep her from falling to the ground. "He's gone. You're safe."

Despite the danger, she believed him. He'd always been her safe place to land, a rock in the turbulent world that she'd hidden from him.

That turbulence had ripped them apart, and he didn't even know it existed.

She couldn't cling to him as though their past hadn't happened. They had needed to come apart three years ago, and they needed to stay apart now. It was the only way to protect him.

Reaching for reserves deep inside, Isabella swallowed her tears then backed away from him. She had grown up strong, had been trained to be strong, and she needed that strength now. She could fall apart later, behind closed doors where nobody could see.

Where Liam couldn't see.

Willing her legs to support her, she rolled onto her hip and moved to stand. The motion shot pain through her leg and shoulder, where she'd crashed to the asphalt road. Biting back a wince, she refused Liam's hand when he jumped up and offered her help.

Standing, she brushed off her black pants and examined a rip in the shoulder of her favorite red shirt. Scrapes marred her skin where asphalt had chewed her up. She twisted her lips wryly. "Well, this won't be wearable again."

When she looked up, Liam was watching with his jaw tight and his lips pressed together. Without addressing her, he pulled out a satellite phone and made a call, probably to the National Park Service or local law enforcement, only speaking directly to her when he asked for her license plate number and car model.

When he was done, he pocketed the phone, crossed his arms over his chest and widened his stance as though he was about to interrogate a suspect. "What were you doing out here alone? Do you have any idea what you've wandered into?" He unwound his arms to point in the direction her SUV had disappeared. "You're a perfect target for him, exactly what he's looking for."

She mimicked his crossed arms, though the motion tore at her shoulder. "I'm well aware. I just sketched the details that his first two victims could remember." She rocked slightly. Now she had details to add to the sketches.

She'd nearly become victim number five.

She cleared her throat to keep her lunch in place.

"And still you're out here." Liam's voice was hard.

As it should be. She had no doubt she'd hurt him when she'd left him, and he had no idea the destruction her decisions had caused to her own heart. For all he knew, she'd callously decided to disappear without an explanation.

But she hadn't. An explanation would have put his career and his life in jeopardy.

While she wanted to fold in on herself to hide from his pain, she forced her spine to remain straight. "I wanted to see where victim four was found. I had to."

Something in Liam's demeanor seemed to crack. While his expression didn't change, his shoulders softened, and his jaw relaxed. He exhaled loudly. "Sometimes seeing it for yourself slays the dragons that try to take up residence in your imagination."

"Exactly." He should know. His job with the FBI had likely given him plenty of nightmare fuel, like Aiyana's job as a deputy had bled into her sleeping hours.

Even Isabella had awakened some nights, chased by stories victims had told as she'd sketched the men and women who had harmed them. She had to be strong as she listened to them, to give them a sense of safety and even hope.

She had to be strong now to keep Liam at arm's length. Leaning on him would only make her want to confess everything. She couldn't protect him if she did that, and she couldn't risk offering him the false hope that they could be together…if he even harbored such hope.

Lord, give me the strength to handle this well. She hadn't expected to feel so strongly about seeing him again, but smelling his familiar scent, hearing his voice…the regret and the pain were so real.

She forced authority into her voice. "I've picked up a few things while doing sketches." She'd also learned a lot of things from him as she'd helped him study for exams back in the day.

She shook off the thought. There was no sense in revisiting happier times. They couldn't be repeated. "This guy doesn't usually grab women out here. He might leave them here, but he takes them in Meadowlark. I'd be the first he tried to kidnap this far out." The world tilted, and she planted her feet.

Liam almost stepped toward her, but it was obvious he stopped himself then pretended not to notice her weakness. "Does he really have a set way he operates? If DNA evidence didn't link him to each of the women, I'd say we had a bunch of random acts. He nabbed the first four in Meadowlark, but he released two, left one to be found in a ritualistic fashion, and hasn't yet revealed the third. Are we sure this isn't a copycat? An opportunist who came out here to scope out the crime scene then considered himself lucky when you drove by? And how did he get out here anyway? It's too remote and too hot for someone to hike."

Gratitude eased her nerves a little. He was following her lead, treating this professionally instead of personally, allowing her to distance herself from the crime as though it hadn't happened to her. It was the only thing that was going to get her through this.

"I have no idea how he got here, but I'm certain he's no copycat. The black mask hasn't been made public."

"Meadowlark PD was holding the DNA evidence close, too. How did you know about that?" She turned to look at him. "In fact, why are you here? The FBI hasn't taken this case, have they?" Surely she'd have heard talk. While she wasn't privy to all of the details, she learned a lot listening during interviews as she drew her sketches. Meadowlark PD had taken point with assistance from the South Dakota Division of Criminal Investigation and the National Park Service's Investigative Services Branch, but she'd heard no mention of the FBI.

"I'm on a task force investigating a gun trafficking ring in the Dakotas. Calista Franklin had ties to a low-level runner in the organization, and I came out here to…" He shrugged, his broad shoulders lifting beneath the gray shirt, which bore damp stains of her earlier tears. "To feel like I'd done all I could, I guess."

He'd always been one to go above and beyond, professionally and personally. No one had ever loved her the way he had. No one had ever gone to such great lengths to show her that she had value and was treasured.

Isabella dropped her gaze to the ground. If only things had been different...

She studied her black flats, which had managed to stay on her feet in the scuffle. They were scratched, and deep drag marks marred the leather. They'd never be the same. Her shoes were—

Shoes. Her head jerked up. "I saw his shoes."

"I'm sorry. What?" Liam's forehead wrinkled. "His shoes?"

"Yeah. When he pulled me out of the car, I managed to get the knit mask up far enough to look beneath it. They were brown boots, and I'm pretty sure the brand was Adventure Bound."

"Never heard of them. And how would you know that?"

She'd never been a fashionista who recognized brands and designers. "I get paid to know things like this. Clothes, shoes, accessories... Sometimes, if a victim describes something distinctive, knowing the brand can be helpful, especially if it's a boutique or rare item. Adventure Bound is a start-up out of Colorado, and they came on my radar a couple of months ago, when a missing hiker was wearing them and searchers were able to track him based on the distinctive logo in the boot's sole. The *A* forms a mountain, and the *B* is stylized to create a cloud and a sunset." The more she discussed work, the more she distanced herself from the horror of the moment. If she could set *self* and *victim* apart, she might survive this day.

Liam eyed her as though she was some sort of alien who had popped up in his world, then walked toward where her car had been, scanning the ground. He shook his head. "No bootprints. The gravel is too packed."

"I don't need them. I know the logo, and it was on the boot's tongue and side."

"It would have helped if we could have taken an impression and gotten a size." He continued to scan the ground, moving slowly toward the side of the road where her SUV had come to rest.

Isabella couldn't help watching. It was as though three years hadn't passed. As though—

Liam stopped suddenly, pulled a glove from his pocket, and knelt to poke something in the dirt.

She stepped closer as he turned to look up, squinting against the sun. "Homemade spike strips." His expression was grim. "Whoever this guy is, he wasn't an opportunist. He set a trap."

It wasn't that he'd doubted the killer was out here, but to have irrefutable proof that the man had methodically planned this? That he'd patiently lain in wait until a victim came along?

And for that victim to be Isabella?

That raised a whole other question... This guy had a type. Had he set a trap and simply hoped a blonde woman would wander alone out into the remote wilderness? Had he spotted Isabella elsewhere and come out ahead of her to set his trap? Or was this something more?

She'd stepped back and was staring past him at the ground, her face more pale than it had been when he'd first seen her.

In another time, he'd have held her close and comforted her. He'd have died for her.

Now? He'd protect her. It was his job.

But he wasn't sure how to handle this situation when it involved a woman who hadn't loved him as much as he'd loved her. Who had callously ripped his world in two without bothering to provide an explanation.

He'd awakened on the morning of his wedding, had showered and dressed only to pick up his phone and find seven missed calls and a text from her college roommate. Isabella's gone.

Liam rocked back on his heels and stared down at the rudimentary spike strip, designed to destroy a tire on contact. A thin, broad strip of wood was overlaid with black rubber cut from what looked to be a car floor mat. Nails of varying length and thickness had been driven up through the device at odd angles, guaranteed to puncture a tire multiple times. Although it lay in pieces, when it had been stretched out into the roadway, it would have been nearly invisible in the shadows of the tall rocks.

He snapped a few photos on his phone, pocketed it, then reached for his satellite phone and made a quick call to the National Park Service to update them with the new information. It was possible the FBI would get involved now that their unsub had crossed state lines to hunt, not just to dump.

They needed to get moving soon. The sun was sliding steadily toward the horizon. The shadows were growing longer, and the land seemed to hold its breath, waiting for the next disaster to strike.

Standing, he slipped the phone into his thigh pocket. "I asked for a BOLO for your SUV. The guy can't get far on a shredded tire. NPS and Meadowlark are on the way. Obviously, I'll stay with you until they arrive." If anyone else was here, he'd have left her to that person's care.

Maybe.

That wasn't worth thinking about now. He stared in the direction of his SUV, on the far side of a rock formation in the shadows, so that his partner would stay cool. "We can go sit in my vehicle with the AC. I have water." She could probably use some.

Isabella was silent.

She was watching him. What was going through her mind? He wanted to ask why she'd cut and run, but this wasn't the time.

He'd practiced so many speeches over the years, usually when he was tired and his guard was down. Some were angry. Some were laced with pain. A few had drifted into pleas for another chance, for answers as to what he could have done to make her stay.

Now that she was in front of him, every word he'd rehearsed fled. He had nothing to say. She'd said everything when she'd vanished.

Still, she was a victim who deserved to be treated with respect. "Come on. I need to check on my partner. He's been cooped up in the vehicle for awhile."

Her head tilted, and blond locks fell over her shoulder. "You left your partner in the car?"

He almost laughed. Yeah, that probably had sounded strange. "I work with a bloodhound named Guthrie. His specialty is cadaver detection."

"A K-9 partner." She walked beside him, her pace slow. "What you always wanted."

Lord, this is weird. The words were the kind he routinely prayed through the day, the kind of random sidebar he often had with the Lord. *Pray without ceasing* meant a running dialogue, so he kept it up.

This really was weird. After three years, the woman who gingerly walked beside him in shoes not made for the trek was a complete stranger...

Yet they knew each other better than he'd ever known anyone else. It was the strangest dichotomy, a sickening blend of familiar and strange that felt surreal. He should be able to talk to her about anything, yet he had nothing to say. He had nothing to *feel*.

As they neared the formation where Calista Franklin's body had been found, Isabella slowed. She stared at the dust-colored rock, then faced east. "I wonder why he brought her out here. Why have her facing the sunrise?"

Was she thinking out loud, or did she want a response? "I'm not on this investigation, so I'm not privileged to the details, but it seems odd. Did the two victims you spoke with mention ritualistic behavior?"

"Not to me, but I haven't seen all of the other case notes. I'd think that would have been a big enough detail to mention to me, though. I mostly got physical details, but..." She turned away from the rock to look at him. "You saw him."

"Only from a distance."

"It might offer more than we have now. I'll sketch what—" She turned left, then right, then her shoulders sank. "I could sketch what you saw, but he took my car. My sketch pads, my tablet, my laptop... He has it all. Even my purse—" Her breath caught. "He has my license, my registration, and my home address." She reached for her pocket and winced. "And my phone." She whipped toward him. "I have a roommate. She's a deputy and can take care of herself, but she needs to be warned. And unless the guy tossed my phone, she can track it because I've shared my location with her."

Liam passed her his satellite phone. "Alert her. Maybe get someone to watch the house in case he goes there, since you're the one who got away. And ask her where your phone is headed, see if it's picked up a tower and can be tracked."

With a nod, Isabella took the phone and walked a few paces away.

Liam surveyed the area, questions dogging him. What was

special about this spot? The killer hadn't kidnapped women from here before, so why now? Why dump Calista then try to take Isabella when he knew law enforcement would be familiar with the place? And where was the third victim?

He looked up the road to the north and to the south. The Badlands covered nearly four hundred square miles, much of it remote, yet the killer had dropped victims one and two within a few miles of this spot and had left Calista's remains here. It made no sense.

Unless he'd connected with something here. Something that kept drawing him back.

If that was the case, then victim number three could be nearby.

"Thanks." Isabella approached, phone extended. "My phone hasn't picked up a tower, so it can't be tracked yet, but Aiyana is going to keep trying. She's staying somewhere else for the next couple of days to take extra precautions at home."

"Is she blonde?" That seemed to be the killer's preferred type. Age and economic status didn't appear to be a factor.

"No."

He pocketed the phone, then started walking at a faster pace toward his SUV. "I want my partner to check the area. I have a feeling. I hope I'm wrong, but I have a feeling." He really didn't want to be right. If Guthrie alerted, that meant there were more bodies, more victims.

As his SUV came into view, Liam reached into his pocket and pressed the remote's button to open the rear liftgate.

Guthrie jumped out and loped toward them, his ears and jowls flopping. The bloodhound was thrilled to be free of his confines and was ready to work, as always. For Guthrie, work truly was life.

As he neared, Isabella stepped back and stood behind Liam's left shoulder.

He nearly smiled. "Guthrie isn't going to attack."

"I know." Her voice was soft, and her eyes never left his partner. "I'm giving the two of you room to work."

Clearly, she'd been around K-9s before. Sometimes, civilians felt the need to treat Guthrie like a pet, but he was a trained FBI agent, just like Liam.

Liam offered her a grateful nod.

Guthrie gave Isabella a curious glance, but he sat at Liam's side, watching for a command. He'd been well trained to lean on Liam for every part of his survival, and his loyalty was unmatched. He'd obey any command immediately and completely.

Liam made eye contact with his partner. *"Suchen."*

Immediately, Guthrie began to sniff the ground around them.

Isabella's whisper came from over his shoulder. "What does that mean?"

"It's German for *seek*. A lot of K-9s are trained on foreign words. It's more tradition than anything else." He stepped away to walk beside Guthrie, gently herding him away from the spot where Calista Franklin had been found. He didn't want any false alerts.

They traversed the area several times, moving between two rock formations. A couple of times, Guthrie showed interest in a patch of ground, but he moved on, ranging farther from the road.

About two hundred yards in, near the base of the second rock formation, he slowed.

Liam stepped back and waited.

Guthrie sniffed the ground and gently nudged it with his nose. It was as though he was careful not to disturb anything. Several seconds passed before he sat and looked expectantly up at Liam.

Passing him a favorite treat, Liam sighed heavily, then guided Guthrie away from the spot and commanded him to lie down.

The K-9 obeyed, happy to settle in with his reward for a job well done.

If only he'd been unsuccessful.

Liam studied the ground. A storm had swept through the area a couple of weeks ago, and that would have obliterated any dig marks. He knelt and investigated the rock formation. Several scratches marred the surface, most of them running perpendicular to the ground.

It was clear a shovel or some other implement had struck it several times.

It was clear he was standing on a grave.

Soft footsteps approached. "He found her, didn't he?" The weight of grief was heavy in Isabella's question.

"Possibly." He pressed his lips together. "Probably. Unless someone else buried a body, then—"

The sound of a vehicle roared up the road, coming toward them at a speed that caused the engine to whine as it was pushed to the limit.

Both he and Isabella whipped toward the sound, and Guthrie stopped chewing his treat to look up.

Isabella spun toward him. "I doubt the Park Service is driving like that."

"No, they're not." And with the vehicle approaching from the direction of his vehicle, which was too far away to make a run for it, they were out of options. "Either someone is out here on a joyride, or our friend has come back to finish the job."

Isabella's face went white.

Liam pulled Guthrie's leash from his pocket, clipped it to his partner's collar, and reached for Isabella's hand. They had no choice. "Run."

THREE

There wasn't time to panic, although her brain screamed that this was the exact right moment to fall apart.

It also wasn't the time to concern herself with their past.

Isabella grasped Liam's outstretched hand and kept pace as he raced away from the road toward a tall rock. At any moment, whoever was approaching would be close enough to spot them. They had to get to cover.

If the driver was the man who'd tried to take her, then they really were in trouble. It wouldn't take long for him to find them. They were the very definition of sitting ducks.

They skidded to a stop at the base of a formation several hundred feet from the one where Guthrie had alerted. They pressed their backs against sun-heated rock and heaved air while Guthrie panted at Liam's feet.

They were directly in the sunlight and it was so, so hot. She was already craving water, and her heart pounded. If help didn't arrive soon, her body might do the killer's work for him.

"What do we do now?" Surely Liam had a plan.

"We wait." He looked down at her, his expression grim and his voice low. "If I have to, I'll protect us."

There was no doubt the possibilities were difficult for him. He'd always been concerned about having to protect civilians in the line of duty. They'd discussed it several times. It was something he'd neither looked forward to nor relished the thought of.

She prayed today was not the day he'd have to take such life-altering actions. *Lord, make that car go away.*

But even as she prayed, the sound of the engine changed. The roar died and faded into a rough hum as the vehicle slowed then stopped only a few hundred feet away. After agonizing moments of idling, the engine shut off.

A car door slammed.

Isabella dug her teeth into her lower lip. Closing her eyes, she fired off wordless prayers, terrified of what might come next.

There was no way this could end well, unless the Park Service arrived in record time.

Beside her, Liam pulled the satellite phone from the thigh pocket of his cargo pants and tapped something into it. He held a finger to his lips and showed her the screen before he hit Send. *Assailant on scene. Victim with me. No cover. 911.*

She nodded. It didn't matter who he was sending it to as long as they responded quickly.

At Liam's feet, Guthrie stared up at him with unwavering attention, clearly waiting for a command. He was quiet, as though he knew life and death depended on their silence.

No sound came from the direction of the vehicle.

The urge to peer around the rock formation was overwhelming, but she didn't dare. They were already on an unknown countdown. There was no need to accelerate it.

Liam kept his head cocked toward the road. His hand rested on the pistol at his side. While Isabella was knotted with tension, he appeared to be relaxed, probably due to years of practice and discipline.

She thanked God he was here. If he hadn't been…

The thought of where she could be right now threatened to close her throat.

Deep breath. Focus on the situation. Keep your wits. She forced herself to think rationally and to let Liam focus on the threat while she sought a way out. Surely there was a place to hide.

Scanning the area, all she saw was more rocks. More space. More...

Wait.

Something was different about the ground around fifty feet away. It was darker, though that could be a trick of the light. This area was lined with crevices that cracked the ground like miniature canyons. Could there be one close enough to shelter them?

She elbowed Liam and tipped her head toward the spot.

He followed her gaze. It seemed like an eternity as he stared into the near distance, probably calculating the risk.

Did they stay where they were and wait for danger to come to them? Or did they risk it all for a minor improvement in their circumstances?

The silence was maddening. If they could hear a footstep, a cough...something, anything to let them know how close the threat was.

It was clear the person lurking in the unknown was no friend. If he was, he'd have called out to them.

It was likely that her would-be kidnapper had returned to finish the job.

But why? Why was he so desperate to get to her, if she was nothing more than a random target?

Was this somehow personal?

Had her past risen up to make a totally unexpected move?

Her mind raced, and her heart followed. Her feet itched to run, yet her back pressed harder against the uneven rock.

Jagged edges dug into her spine, shooting twinges of pain through her tender shoulder.

If only she'd gone straight home instead of running this fool's errand to a crime scene in the middle of nowhere.

Liam's hand brushed hers, putting the brakes on her spinning thoughts. When she looked up, he pointed toward what might prove to be nothing more than a shallow ditch and gave her a terse nod.

He wanted them to run.

With a deep, fortifying breath, Isabella returned the nod and peeled her back from the rock face.

When Liam made an upward sweeping motion with his hand, Guthrie rose, all attention on him. The K-9's instant obedience said he'd follow Liam anywhere.

Something about that settled peace over Isabella. Guthrie trusted Liam without question. He trusted Liam with his life.

She could stand to be a little more like that with God, couldn't she?

Yesterday, she'd read a verse in Psalms about him knowing every day of her life from beginning to end. That was something she was going to have to trust now. Even though she'd gotten herself and Liam into this situation with her bad decision, God wasn't caught off guard. From the beginning of time, He'd seen this moment coming, and He knew the end result.

Okay, God. You've got this, no matter what happens next.

Like Guthrie, she had to put her eyes on Someone who had more wisdom and knowledge than herself. She had to focus and not get distracted.

Gently, Liam took her hand and drew her in front of him, her back to his chest, his hands on her biceps. He was close that she could feel his chest move as he breathed. He leaned forward and spoke directly into her ear, his words barely more than a whisper. "On three." He let go of her arms. "One…two…three."

Without looking to the right or to the left, Isabella ran. Away from shelter. Away from protection. Into the open where every step might be her last.

He'd had no idea Isabella could run that fast.

Without looking back, Liam followed Isabella's swift footsteps to their salvation, which might be nothing more than a shallow hole in the ground that would leave them trapped.

Beside him, Guthrie kept pace, alternating between looking ahead and looking up at Liam. If there was one thing he didn't have to worry about, it was his partner being right beside him at every step.

Every step which seemed to take him farther away from their destination instead of closer to it. In the wavering heat and with adrenaline pumping, it seemed the crevice in the ground moved farther away with every inch they traveled.

It had better not have been a mirage, a trick of the heat and the fading light. Surely not. Surely…

Isabella skidded to a stop. Without looking back, she took a deep breath and jumped, disappearing into the ground.

Liam skidded to a halt beside where she'd vanished.

The crack in the earth was about four feet wide and evenly spaced from top to bottom. The sides were steep and weathered, smooth in some places but craggy in others. The ground was fairly level at the bottom, and the entire crevice was about five feet deep. Isabella crouched below him, looking up.

Guthrie could make the jump easily, and so could he.

A quick glance behind him revealed no figure running toward them, so he motioned for Guthrie to make the leap, then followed his partner into what was little more than a ditch.

He landed with a thud and knelt beside Isabella, who rested her hand on his arm and mouthed, *Are you okay?*

He couldn't help it. His eyebrow arched in wry amusement at the irony. *She* was worried about *him*?

He nodded then took inventory of their surroundings.

It was warmer down here and still. The hot air had settled and was unstirred by any breeze from above.

It would be difficult to shelter in the crevice for long. The space felt like they were being baked in an industrial oven.

The deep crack in the dry ground carved a meandering path that ran almost parallel to the road several hundred yards to their right before angling away from it.

Which way should they go? Help would come with the Park Service toward the road, but anyone searching for them in the wilderness would assume that was the path they'd taken. Besides, it was instinct in most people to go right when given an option. He hoped Isabella's assailant would follow that instinct.

It was better to go left, deeper into the wilderness, and to wait for help. He had his satellite phone. Surely someone would reach out when they arrived on the scene.

He gave a quick glance at the phone. Though his text appeared to have sent, there was no response. Hopefully, it had been received. He didn't want anyone racing up to an active scene without warning, and they needed the Park Service to put a rush on reaching them. This had escalated into much more than his initial call had indicated since the threat had returned.

Pocketing the phone, he pointed to the left, where the crevice hooked a sharp turn about a hundred feet away, angling away from the setting sun. Ushering Isabella and Guthrie ahead of him, Liam hurried forward, careful to keep his head below the rim. He rested his hand on his sidearm as he followed them, focused on hearing any sounds from above.

His back ached from hunching forward as they ran. His breaths came quickly in the heat, and his heart pounded with the exertion.

Ahead of him, Guthrie panted with his tongue lolling as he followed closely behind Isabella, who was also suffering the effects of their situation and surroundings. They could go a little while without water, but not long. The conditions were harsh, and adrenaline coupled with the hot air and their rapid pace would sap them quickly.

Had he known this was going to happen, he'd have grabbed his bag out of the SUV, where he carried Guthrie's supplies and extra water.

But who could have anticipated this?

They rounded the bend and kept going for a few minutes before he reached for Isabella's shirt and urged her to slow. Without landmarks, it was tough to tell how far they'd traveled, but he didn't dare lift his head above ground level to get his bearings. He simply had to trust that they'd put some distance between them and whoever had arrived at the crime scene. They needed to take a minute to catch their breaths while moving at a slower place, or they'd burn out quickly.

Isabella stopped, and Liam gestured for her to sit, then silently commanded Guthrie to lie down.

As Isabella sank to the ground and leaned forward over her bent knees, Guthrie settled beside her, not quite touching her. He was alert, watching Liam and occasionally looking around the area. He panted and eyed Liam, expecting water that wasn't available.

Liam hated failing his partner. He sat against the opposite wall and stretched his legs out as far as he could, then scratched Guthrie's ears. "Help will be here soon, buddy."

He continued whispering reassurances to the K-9 while he surveyed Isabella. "You okay over there?"

For a moment, she didn't move. Maybe he'd spoken too softly, but he didn't dare raise his volume. After a moment, she lifted her head and looked at him.

Her normally fair cheeks were pink, and it was clear the heat was taking a toll. "I'm fine," she barely whispered. "When's help arriving?"

He'd hoped she wouldn't ask. He pulled the satellite phone from his pocket and glanced at the screen. A new message beacon flashed. *OTW. Hang tight.*

On the way. There was no estimated time of arrival, although the message had been sent five minutes earlier. He tried to keep his disappointment from showing as he showed the message to Isabella.

She was not as successful as he'd been in hiding her emotions. Her expression fell. She looked down at Guthrie and whispered, "Can I pet him?"

Liam nodded. Over the years, he'd recognized over and over again that Guthrie was much more than a partner. He was a family member, a friend and would have made an excellent therapy dog. His intuition and gentle nature were traits that had endeared him to Liam over the past couple of years since they'd been paired up. How many nights had he sat on his living room floor much like this, letting the day fall away as he scratched Guthrie's floppy ears or rubbed that soft belly?

As Isabella tentatively petted Guthrie's side, his partner looked up at him.

Liam gestured his permission, and Guthrie wriggled until his back rested along Isabella's leg.

She visibly relaxed, her attention focused on Guthrie.

Around them, the silence weighed heavily, broken only by Guthrie's panting.

Liam would give anything to hear sirens in the distance. Without lifting his head above the rim to look, there was no way to know if they'd been followed or if help had arrived.

So he waited, ears tuned to the world above, hand resting near his sidearm, and eyes focused on Isabella.

He'd honestly never expected to see her again. Her departure had been so sharp, so sudden. No communication. No explanation. He'd awakened on a day he'd looked forward to almost since he'd met her, a day that should have been the happiest of his life, only to have it turn into a nightmare—it sometimes felt like he'd still not awakened from it. Here she sat now, a victim. A stranger who had once owned his heart. Sometimes, it felt like she still did, only she'd gripped it in an iron fist until she'd crushed it and bled it dry.

She didn't look any different. The same hazel eyes that had looked into his with open affection gazed at Guthrie. The same blond hair that he'd once run his fingers through fell forward over her shoulder. Time had been kind to her. She could have stepped out of one of her art history classes an hour ago.

How could that face and those eyes mask a heart so cruel? Had she lied to him for their entire relationship? Had she used him for...for what? As many nights as he'd lain awake and tried to puzzle out her motive for vanishing, he'd never been able to come up with anything that made sense. Everything had been fine...until it hadn't been. She'd simply walked away without bothering to offer any explanation, and despite his best efforts, he'd never heard another word.

He wasn't about to ask her any questions now. There was too much happening. Once he handed her over to the Park

Service, he'd walk away, even though doing so would leave him without answers.

He looked toward the sky, which slipped into a deeper blue by the minute.

There was nowhere for either of them to go. She couldn't evade his questions if he put them out there. He could ask for answers and put to rest all of the horrible thoughts and conjectures that still raced around in his head.

Except he needed to be focused. To be listening. To be prepared if—

Guthrie lifted his head and stood, sniffing the air.

Isabella looked from his partner to Liam, her brow furrowed.

Something changed in the atmosphere around them, something he couldn't quite discern, but the air felt disturbed, as though—

Overhead, footsteps crunched.

Liam reached for his weapon as a shadow fell over them.

FOUR

Isabella's heart raced. Bile burned her throat. Terror heated her skin.

They were out of places to run.

She buried her face in her knees and waited to die.

As Liam crouched and drew his sidearm, she knew fear like never before. Horror movies weren't real, but this must be how the characters would have felt when they were hunted and trapped, waiting for a faceless enemy to step out of the shadows and rip away their lives.

"Well." A woman's voice rained down over them. "You sure dug yourself a hole this time, huh, Barringer?" Sarcasm laced the words from above. "And it looks like you're going to need me to rescue you."

She jerked her head up and squinted against the light. What was happening? Who was—

"Jenna." Liam sagged into a seated position and holstered his sidearm. "What are you doing here? I didn't realize other members of the DGTF were in the immediate area."

"Surprise. And we've brought along a few locals. The area's cleared. It's safe to surface."

Obviously, this was friend and not foe.

Fear ebbed so quickly that tears rushed in to fill the void.

They were safe. Help had arrived and had hopefully taken her would-be kidnapper into custody.

If they had, she could put this ordeal behind her and so could the town of Meadowlark. With the last of her strength, she pivoted to look up toward the voice.

Jenna looked down at them, her blue eyes holding an odd tension that her amused words covered. Her chestnut-brown hair was pulled back in a ponytail, and her tight jaw seemed to betray the smile she'd pasted on. She was relieved, but she was also concerned.

Beside her, a German shepherd peered over the edge, panting happily at the sight of Guthrie, whose tail wagged with recognition and joy.

"Did you guys find our suspect?" Liam's voice was tight.

Jenna's face fell as she looked away at something in the distance. "No."

Isabella's hopes tumbled with Jenna's expression. They might be rescued, but this was far from over. "Was he here when you got here?"

"No," Jenna said, "but there's a small silver SUV parked by the road. Based on the intel we got on the drive over, I assume it's Isabella's. NPS is securing the scene."

Sinking next to Guthrie, Isabella rested her hand on his warm side and looked up at Jenna. "That's my car. He took off in it when Liam showed up and rescued me."

Somewhere out there, he was still on the hunt. Still searching.

What was she going to do?

Jenna's blue gaze shifted to Isabella, pulling her from her spiraling fears. "Hi, I'm Officer Jenna Morrow. This is my partner Augie, and we're your knights in shining armor." She pulled a backpack from her shoulder and dug into it. "And I come bearing gifts."

Liam stood. "Tell me your snack machine contains water today."

"Water and..." She rooted around in the bag. "Peanut M&M's." Crouching, she passed Liam a bottle of water and a collapsible bowl, then handed Isabella another water and a yellow bag of candy. "Only one package of M&M's though, and it's for the lady." She turned to Liam. "You're on your own. I packed light today. Figured water was more important than sugar."

Who cared about candy? Isabella grabbed the water bottle, twisted the cap and gulped. It was warm but she didn't care. It was wet. Even after only a few sips, her body like it was returning to the land of the living.

"Slow down." Liam had leaned down and was pouring water into a bowl for Guthrie, but he seemed to instinctively know what she was doing. "Gulp too much too fast and you'll regret it." As Guthrie lapped at the water in the bowl, Liam straightened and took several long sips from what was left in the bottle. "How did you find us?"

"Cheyenne—our tech analyst," she added, looking at Isabella for a moment, "tracked your sat phone. We had you within about fifty feet. Didn't want to call out in case you were in trouble." Jenna crouched at the rim of the crevice, rested her hand on Augie's back, and scanned the walls. "Think you can climb out if I lend a hand, or do we need to get a whole rock climbing rig brought in because you've gone soft?"

"Pretty sure I can climb out." Liam looked over at Isabella. "If Jenna helps from the top and I boost from down here, do you think you can climb out?"

Did he think she was weak? That she didn't regularly go to the gym to combat long days in her car and at her desk? She took another sip of water and swallowed a rising fear-fueled anger along with it. Now that they were safe, the full effects of what had almost happened to her reared their ugly heads.

Liam didn't deserve for her to take it out on him. If anything, his anger should be scorching her right now. She was the one who'd wronged him...although she had done so for all of the right reasons.

Checking her emotions, she lowered the bottle to her side. "I can manage, but what about Guthrie? He's a tall boy, but I'm pretty sure he's not going to be climbing any walls." While the crevice was under six feet deep, it would be tough to lift or pull the K-9 to the surface without hurting him.

"I'll have a harness brought over." Jenna tapped on a satellite phone similar to Liam's. "Daniel's here. He'll bring one out of his SUV."

"Perfect." Liam drained his water, then crushed the bottle and shoved it into his pocket.

Jenna rocked back on her heels and surveyed the surrounding land. "I'm curious how he got out here in the first place? I mean, sure, he could have hidden a car behind any of these pillars, but why risk leaving his vehicle behind? And why bring hers back when it could be covered in his DNA and prints?"

"I don't think taking her SUV was planned. I showed up and threw him off." Liam planted his hands on his hips. "There are a lot of places to hide out here. He could have staged his car near where he disabled Isabella's and then brought hers back to retrieve his."

Boy, did she hope he'd only come back to get his car and not to stalk her further. Maybe he'd give up on her now that she had caused him trouble. He'd nearly been caught trying to take her, which meant he'd probably be more careful when he found a new woman to prey upon.

Her gut twisted. The last thing she wanted was for someone else to fall victim to this man's sickness. *God, reveal who he is. Let him be found. Stop what he's doing before he hurts someone else.*

"Isabella?" Jenna's head tilted. "Is that your name?" She studied Isabella with narrowed, curious eyes. "Isn't that the—"

"Somebody call for a lift?" Two more people appeared at the top of the crevice. A young man wearing a National Park Service uniform had been the one to speak.

Beside him, a slightly older man with a defined jaw, tousled dark blond hair, and green eyes peered over the edge. He shook his head with a cross between a smirk and a frown. "Let's get you two out of here" As he spoke, his hands worked on attaching a rope to a harness. "Isabella, are you okay?"

"I am."

The man tossed the harness to Liam. "Good. We're going to make sure you stay that way."

She wanted to buy his reassurance, but how? That man was still out there, still hunting, and since he'd been in her car with her registration and her wallet…he knew exactly where she lived.

"How about you don't ask any more questions?" Liam turned away from Jenna's knowing gaze. He closed the back of his SUV, where Guthrie slurped water from his built-in bowl in air-conditioned comfort. "There are a lot of women in the world named Isabella." And he didn't need Jenna digging into his connection to this one.

Where was Isabella anyway? He scanned the area. Several official vehicles lined the road, while Daniel's and Jenna's vehicles sat next to his. Up the road, out of sight behind a rock formation, the National Park Service's Investigative Services Branch was securing Isabella's SUV and the area around it, collecting evidence before they called in a wrecker to move it. Given that they had a likely serial killer on their hands—if Guthrie's alert earlier would reveal the burial site of the third victim—the ISB were being exceptionally thorough.

But where was Isabella? Daniel had whisked her away to be checked out by medial personnel who had arrived on scene. It had been a good fifteen minutes since she'd walked away with the head of the Dakota Gun Task Force.

Although Liam trusted Daniel with his life, he had no idea who the other people on scene were. He had no idea who the kidnapper was—and for all anyone knew, he was hiding in plain sight.

Liam turned away from Jenna and stepped toward the road, scanning each individual vehicle and each person moving between them.

There. Isabella sat on the back bumper of a tricked-out SUV made to tackle any terrain while two paramedics hovered around her. She was talking to an investigator while a medic doctored the road rash on her shoulder where she'd hit the ground earlier. From this distance, she appeared to be calm, but her face had grown pale again as the heat and adrenaline had dissipated.

The two paramedics were decked out in short-sleeved dark green jumpsuits. They wore surgical masks and baseball caps that kept the late afternoon sun out of their eyes. A third man stood beside the SUV in jeans and a National Park Service jacket, also wearing a baseball cap and a mask, apparently supervising the situation.

A couple of car lengths away, Daniel was on the phone, watching the scene with a frown on his face. Whoever he was talking to, he either didn't like what they were saying or he was processing information through an analytical filter that made him one of the most skilled investigators Liam had ever met.

Liam turned his attention back to the man and woman working with Isabella. The lack of visible facial features set Liam on edge. The man who had tried to kidnap her had worn a ski mask. He could be lingering anywhere.

Although he'd be a fool if he was.

The sun would set in an hour or so, and the temperature would drop. Liam wanted nothing more than to be out of the Badlands, where it would be pitch black in no time. When darkness fell, shadows would creep out from behind every rock and rise up from every crevice. His imagination would go into overload.

Even more importantly, he needed to get Isabella to safety so he could turn her over to someone else before she tugged any more of his heartstrings.

Jenna stepped closer, crowding his personal space. "That's her, isn't it?"

"Like I said, plenty of people are named—"

"You're evading the question." She poked him in the chest a little too hard. "I've seen you around victims before, and you've never looked at any of them like you're looking at her. Sure, you take care of people. You protect them and put them ahead of yourself, especially when they're in crisis, but you don't act the way you're acting now. You're *too* concerned." With a knowing nod, Jenna stepped back and gave him room to breathe. "That's the girl you told me and Cheyenne about that time we were all up for days tracking down that lead in—"

"Stop." He couldn't handle the third degree. Not now. "That woman over there was nearly abducted today by a man who terrorized two women, definitely murdered another, and has likely killed a fourth whose body Guthrie may have found earlier. Given the situation, my personal life is the last thing you should be worried about." He poked her bicep the way she'd jabbed his chest. "And don't go talking to Cheyenne about this either."

"Too late."

Liam rolled his eyes and bit his tongue. Jenna and Cheyenne, the technical expert on the DGTF, were close. It seemed they told one another everything. One night, he'd been working on a records search with the two of them. It had been late and he'd been exhausted. Boredom and lack of sleep had weakened the walls he usually built around his personal life. He'd stumbled into their camaraderie and had trusted them with his story. Neither of them had ever said another word about it.

Until now.

Of course it would be Jenna on scene when he called for help while Isabella was with him. That's how it went, wasn't it?

Speaking of… "I asked you earlier and you never answered. What are you and Daniel doing here? I thought I was the only one checking out this lead."

"We were coming back from Fargo where we followed up on another lead. We weren't too far away when Cheyenne tipped us off that you were looking for help."

So they had something solid to go on in the gun trafficking case, the very case that had led the ATF to form the Dakota Gun Task Force.

This was exactly what he needed to keep his mind off of Isabella. Leaning against the rear bumper of his SUV, he crossed his arms. "What kind of lead?" Maybe they were finally getting somewhere. He loved his teammates, and they'd become close in a short amount of time, but it was tough pulling double duty on his day-to-day work for the FBI while also running leads for the DGTF.

The Dakota Gun Task Force had been formed a few months after Plains City K-9 Detective Kenyon Graves had been killed in an explosion while talking to an informant who had information on the gun trafficking ring. His death had rocked the tight-knit department at Plains City. The death of the informant, who had been working hard to turn her life around after years of walking on the wrong side of the law, had been yet another blow.

The investigation into Kenyon's and the informant's deaths had yielded evidence that the ring was much larger than authorities had initially suspected. When another Plains City detective, West Cole, had uncovered a huge stash of weapons that were bound for both North and South Dakota, it was clear that more needed to be done.

Given that Plains City PD had proof that the ring was operating across state lines, the ATF had stepped in and formed a task force comprised of K-9 officers from state, local, and federal agencies to investigate and shut down the ring. Not only were they trying to get weapons traffickers off the streets, they were also trying to get justice for a fallen detective's murder.

The DGTF had been on the case for over four months, and all they had was a loose connection to the Plains City Pizzeria, where it seemed guns were being stored without the owner's knowledge, and two dead traffickers who were brutally slaughtered by someone higher up the food chain after West intercepted the shipment they were transporting. The investigation had led to another gunrunner, and the team was digging into his background.

They desperately needed more.

"What's in Fargo? Did we get somewhere with that name

Lucy got for us?" Fargo PD Officer Lucy Lopez and her K-9 partner, Piper, had located a new recruit in the ring, Nick Landon. Nick had told them about Brandon Jones, who was a bigwig trafficker, and knew quite a bit about their movements, mostly because Jones was prone to bragging.

Jenna watched Isabella and the EMTs. "Are you sure you don't want to talk about—"

"Jenna." Liam put enough force behind her name to shut her down once and for all.

With a sigh and an eye roll, she dragged her attention to him. "Fine. We'll talk business, but this isn't over." Tilting her head, she gave him a hard look but kept on talking. "Cheyenne did some digging and found out that Brandon Jones bounces between two homes, one in Plains City and one in Fargo. He's also got a brother, Hal Jones. She's looking into him now. This Brandon guy isn't too bright. He seems to view himself as a wheeler and a dealer, wants to be a high roller old-school mobster type. You know, a real celebrity kingpin. Likes to have his picture taken with the guys lower on the rung than him. Makes him feel famous."

Liam allowed himself a smile. "Ah, our favorite kind of suspect. The guy with enough swagger to talk too much. The kind of guy who thinks he's smarter than 'the cops' so he can flaunt himself right out in the open."

"Bingo." Jenna tapped her temple. "But I think there's more going on. Daniel was on the phone with Cheyenne and a couple of his ATF buddies on the drive out here and didn't have much time to talk to me when I was relaying intel about your situation to him. I'm guessing we're due a team meeting, an all-hands-on-deck thing, so be prepared to head back to HQ in Plains City soon."

Nodding slowly, Liam looked to where Isabella had been

talking to the medics. Soon was when he'd like to get out of here.

The paramedics were packing up their SUV and chatting.

He took a step closer to their vehicle, frantically searching faces.

But he couldn't find Isabella's. He scanned the crowd again, looking for her, but she was nowhere to be seen.

She was gone.

FIVE

"I'm really fine. There's no need for anyone to call an ambulance." Isabella walked beside the man who had been supervising the medics tending to her shoulder. In the few tenths of a mile between where her SUV had been abandoned and the original crime scene, nearly a dozen Park Service investigators and first responders worked the area. "I don't need to be transported. I bruised my shoulder. Otherwise, I'm fine."

The agent walking beside her had introduced himself as Reese, and had asked to see the location where her car had gone off the road and where she'd been thrown to the ground. He wanted her to talk him through the incident.

She wasn't sure she could, not without support. The only person she knew here was Liam, and feeling safe with him probably wasn't a good thing.

"Ma'am." He had a deep Southern drawl that was tough to place. Could be Texas, maybe lower Alabama, even northern Virginia. The Park Service assigned people in a way similar to the way the military did, so he could have been from anywhere.

He adjusted his baseball cap over longish dark hair and kept walking with purpose, nodding to an investigator as they passed. He still wore the surgical mask he'd had on when she was with the medics. It was identical to theirs. "I understand, but the medic recommended it and I'm all for taking precautions." He stayed a step ahead of her as they walked toward where her SUV had spun out. "Before you go though, I'd like to ask you a few questions about what happened and to get another look at the scene. I'd like to hear your statement as well."

"I already talked to an FBI agent, Carl Givens. He's waiting to talk to me."

"We'll head his way next." Agent Reese was no-nonsense.

She'd prefer someone with a gentler manner. Not that she *felt* like a victim, but she was definitely one harsh word away from melting down. A girl didn't nearly wreck her car, get kidnapped, and have to flee into the wilderness every day. It wouldn't take much to shove her over the edge. But she needed to get to her SUV and retrieve her sketchbook, and if Agent Reese was heading there now, she'd accompany him. She wanted to draw what she remembered while it was fresh and go back over the witness sketches from earlier.

Still…they were straying from the safety of the law enforcement crowd. "I'd like to have Agent Barringer with me also, if that's okay." She stopped walking and turned to look to where Liam had been standing by his SUV, talking to Officer Morrow. Her view was blocked by the tall rock formation he'd parked his SUV behind before she had arrived on the scene.

"Certainly." He pulled his phone from his pocket and typed something into it. "I've got a guy over there who will send him this way."

"Thank you."

"Yes, ma'am. You've had a difficult day. Anything to help you feel more comfortable." He slowed as they neared the dead area between her abandoned SUV and the place where she'd run off the road.

They were approaching a tall rock formation on their side of the road. Across the asphalt, another large crevice like the one they'd hidden in meandered into the distance between other tall rocks, branching off into multiple directions. As the sun sank lower, the shadows grew longer, making the rocks look like sleeping giants, waiting for darkness so they could awaken and stalk the Badlands.

She shivered. "I'm ready for this to be over."

"I'm sure." Reese slowed, watching the area, his head swinging back and forth, probably looking for threats.

She needed to talk, to put words into the space between them so that they'd chase away the dark shadows in her imagination. The man who had grabbed her could be anywhere, behind any rock, in any spot carved into the ground. He could jump out at any moment and drag her away.

In this vast wilderness, they might never find her body. She pulled in a shuddering breath. "I need them to hand over my sketchbook and my tablet. I hope they don't hold them as evidence. Can you help with that?" The sooner she could get her hands on them, the more she'd feel like herself.

Reese stopped walking. Shoving his hands into his pockets, he paced past her, staring toward her abandoned SUV, which sat out of sight around a slight curve. "Sketches?" His voice was low. Something about the gravelly tone crawled down her spine. "What sketches?"

"Of the man who kidnapped those two women. Who—"

Reese cursed, his back growing rigid. Whirling toward her, he closed the distance between them, his fists balled at his sides.

Fists covered in burn scars.

Isabella almost choked on the fear that burst up from her lungs. She dropped her gaze to his boots.

The Adventure Bound logo seemed to shout a warning.

A scream caught in her throat. Her mind ordered her legs to run, but they refused to move. She was stuck in a nightmare, the air as thick as wool, her feet encased in concrete, her lungs empty.

She couldn't tear her gaze away from those hands, the ones that had tried to take her away. The hands that had killed once.

The hands that would kill again.

His right palm shot out like a coiled rattlesnake, and a silver braided chain slipped from his shirtsleeve. It was the same bracelet one of the victims had described to her earlier.

His scarred fingers clamped around her wrist. "Not a sound. Not…one…sound," he hissed, and jerked her arm. "We're—"

"Hey!" The shout came from behind Reese. "What are you doing?"

Cursing, Reese hesitated, his grip on Isabella's wrist tightening until throbbing pain shot into her hand.

This was her chance. With a guttural cry, she threw her full weight against him, desperate to knock him off balance. She could end all of this here. Now.

Reese stumbled backward as more shouts joined the first.

Cursing louder, he flung her away from him.

Isabella stumbled, crashing into the rock formation before dropping to her knees. The air forced out of her lungs in a gasp. Pain shot through her injured shoulder.

By the time she regained her breath and scrambled to her feet, the killer had vanished.

This was all his fault. He never should have taken his eyes off of her.

"Get Augie!" Liam shouted at Jenna as he raced away. Her partner was trained in suspect apprehension. If Isabella was in trouble and Augie could get a scent or sight of the man who'd grabbed Isabella, they had a chance of capturing him today.

As Jenna ran for her SUV, Liam raced toward the sound of Isabella's scream and of shouting voices. Rounding the curve, the first thing he saw was Isabella, pointing across the road. She was pale and visibly shaken. Several park rangers and investigators sprinted in the direction she indicated and disappeared into a crevice much like the one he and Isabella had hidden in a short time ago.

How had so much happened so fast?

Sprinting faster, he came to a quick stop beside Isabella, his feet sliding on gravel and nearly pitching him into her.

A female ranger reached out to steady him. The look on his face must have screamed *panic* to her. She laid a hand on his shoulder. "She's okay."

"She's right." Isabella pulled away from another park ranger, who was holding her elbow. Her voice shook, and tears streaked the dust and sweat that covered her cheeks. She slid her feet farther apart in an obvious effort to balance herself and extricated her elbow from the ranger's grasp. "I'm fine."

"You're not fine." As more shouts came from across the road, Liam put an arm around her shoulders and guided her toward his SUV. It was past time to get her out of here and to somewhere safe. Everything else could wait. "Let's go."

As they walked toward his SUV, Jenna raced by with Augie, not even acknowledging them as she rushed to the scene.

Whatever was happening, the Park Service and Jenna could handle it. His main interest was in making sure Isabella didn't find herself in the crosshairs again.

Because she was clearly a target.

FBI Agent Carl Givens approached and fell in beside them. "What happened?"

Biting his lip, Liam kept his mouth shut. Givens had been in charge of the entire scene. It was his people investigating. How had their unsub sneaked through the lines to reach Isabella again?

Beneath his arm, Isabella trembled as she walked, but she hadn't moved to pull away from him. If she was in her right mind, she'd probably have shaken him off long ago.

When she spoke, her voice was steadier than before, though a slight tremor ran through her words. "I don't know exactly. I was..." She waved a shaky hand toward the medics' SUV as it came into sight around the curve. "I was with the EMTs, and he was there the whole time, like he was supervising. He said his name was Reese, but then when I mentioned my sketchbook, he turned violent." She turned toward her car. "My sketchbook. My tablet. If the kidnapper didn't take them, I'd like to have those, not have them go into evidence. Please."

Agent Givens nodded. "We can get those to you."

"Big of you." Sarcasm dripped from Liam's words. He couldn't help it. Givens had let the scene get away from him, had allowed a killer to get near his chosen target.

Just as quickly as his anger flared, it cooled. Liam had stepped away from Isabella as well. Daniel had taken a phone call and walked off alone. Jenna had been updating him on their other case. When it came to Isabella, they had all dropped the ball.

Somehow, he was the one who'd fumbled the worst. He'd been the first on scene. The first to see her in danger. The one who should have been the most vigilant, who should have taken responsibility for her until she was safe. If anyone should be on the sharp end of someone's pointed anger, it was him. "Sorry," he mumbled to Givens, and the word left an unfamiliar taste on his tongue.

It was a word he wished Isabella would say.

As Givens acknowledged the apology with a tip of his head, Liam shook off that thought. This wasn't about the past. This was about someone in danger now, no matter who she was, and he needed either to focus or hand her over to someone else who could protect her.

The thought crawled across his skin. Even though he wanted to get out of here faster than he could say his own name, even though she'd cut him to the core three years earlier and the scar was still raw, he couldn't bring himself to walk away. He might never sleep again, worrying about whether or not someone else had dropped the ball...

The way he had.

Isabella stumbled, and he realized he'd tugged her tightly against him. He relaxed his hold but didn't pull his arm away. If a killer thought he was going to get to someone under Liam's protection again, he had a world of hurt coming his way.

Givens slowed as they neared Liam's SUV. "When he fled, he took off deeper into the Badlands. I'd like to say we could catch him, but that crevice runs in about eight different directions. It's likely where he took off the first time he vanished. We've called in ATVs and air support, but he could get pretty far and hide anywhere about now."

"And if our K-9 can't get a scent or sight on him, then we've got nothing." Liam opened the front passenger door of his SUV and helped Isabella inside. "He made his way out here and only took Isabella's SUV earlier as a quick means of escape. He got out here somehow, so he must have a vehicle stashed not too far away."

"Can't be too close, or we'd have spotted it." Givens

handed a card to Liam. "Let me know where you take Ms. Whitmore and I'll complete an interview with her when you're in a secure location."

Liam pocketed the card. He had a pretty good idea of where he was headed, although Isabella wouldn't like it.

It didn't matter. He was the one behind the wheel.

He closed the SUV's door without revealing his plans to Isabella then turned as a defeated Jenna strode up with Augie. She merely shook her head. They'd come away with nothing.

Daniel was behind her with his Great Dane partner, Dakota, at his side. Daniel's expression was as dark as the growing shadows.

Their task force leader planted his hands on his hips, his green eyes hard. Like his partner, Dakota seemed to take in everything around them, looking up at Daniel every few seconds to watch for a command.

Daniel motioned for Dakota to sit without taking his gaze away from Jenna. "No dice?"

"No. There were too many people for Augie to scent him, and he was gone in that crevice before we ever got there. There's no telling where he is." She looked defeated, as though she'd failed him.

Daniel offered a sympathetic expression. "It's not your fault."

"It's not." Liam echoed the sentiment. Sometimes things simply didn't work the way they wished. "Thanks for trying."

Jenna leaned down to scratch Augie's ears, then walked away to let him rest in her SUV.

"She'll beat herself up for a bit, but she'll recover." Daniel watched Jenna go before he turned to Liam. "Hard to believe you were out here at the exact moment that Isabella Whitmore would need someone."

It was definitely hard to believe. Things would have been much different if he hadn't headed out here to follow a lead that hadn't provided any fruit for the DGTF. In a wild turn of events, his presence had blown wide open the serial kidnapper-killer case for Meadowlark PD.

It had also saved Isabella's life.

The wildest part was, Daniel didn't know the half of what a "coincidence" this actually was. The DGTF task force leader had never heard Liam's story of being literally left at the altar.

He wasn't about to tell it now. "I don't believe in coincidence." He'd wrestled with his faith after Isabella had left. Ultimately, after a lot of long talks with his dad and some even longer solo camping trips in the Black Hills, he'd grown closer to God and had strengthened his faith in the wake of anger, confusion, and grief.

Not that he didn't feel pain and anger on occasion. He just knew where to take those emotions when they hit. Today was going to be one of those days when he needed to hand those emotions over to God in a big way.

Daniel leaned forward slightly, watching the side-view mirror of Liam's SUV. He was probably using the reflection to see Isabella, who sat in the front seat with her head against the headrest and her eyes closed. "Not a coincidence?" He straightened and stared at the sinking sun. "The longer I walk this walk, the more I see things that *aren't coincidence*. The only way things make sense is..." He trailed off.

Daniel was fairly new in his relationship with Christ, and he was learning to see things through a different kind of lens. It often awed or quieted his normally brusque manner when God did something he viewed as "surprising."

After a pause, something in Daniel's posture seemed to reset. "What's your plan?"

It was a quick shift in thought, but that was how ATF Special Agent Daniel Slater operated. While he was in charge of the Dakota Gun Task Force, he allowed his agents autonomy and was handing Liam the lead on whatever happened next with Isabella's case.

The problem was, Liam didn't have a plan. It was all popping in on the fly. The only thing he knew was that the best place to run when things were in flux was home. "HQ is about an hour and a half away. I know she'll be safe there. We can regroup and see about getting the FBI officially involved, since it's getting clear this guy is crossing state lines repeatedly and he's not done yet. We need a recovery team out here, too. We got caught up in him trying to take Isabella, but we've got to remember that Guthrie hit on human remains over there." He pointed toward where Guthrie had alerted. The event felt like days ago. "I want to know what's going on, and I want to be put on this case if it goes federal."

"Recovery and crime scene teams are en route. They were told to stand down until the situation was settled here, either because the suspect was in custody or because the scene was secure. They'll set a detail on the scene and do a dig where Guthrie alerted at daybreak tomorrow. It's too dangerous tonight, and it would be too easy to miss something crucial." Daniel stopped surveying the area to pin his gaze on Liam. "We're having an all-hands team meeting at HQ this evening. I'll lead the way back, you follow me, and Jenna will take the rear so that nobody can come at you and Isabella Whitmore without going through us. We'll get everybody together and parcel out duties on the task force so that you can focus on what's happening here. I have a meeting this evening with an old friend of my dad's, but then Jenna and I can back you up if needed."

Liam tilted his head, but he kept his mouth shut. Jenna

had said they were headed from Fargo back to Plains City when they heard he was in trouble. What could they have learned that was so important that they'd needed to get to headquarters?

He circled his SUV and reached for the door handle. He couldn't stop thinking the worst. Either they had a break in the case...

Or the smugglers had killed again.

SIX

"What are you doing out here? The meeting is in one of the conference rooms." Plains City PD Officer Jack Donadio stopped beside Liam in the hallway near a memorial wall for fallen officers from the PCPD. The police department occupied the lower floors of the building in downtown Plains City, and the ATF held court upstairs. Liam had been headed for the elevator when the memorial had drawn him.

With Isabella safely tucked away in his office, he'd needed to take a minute to remind himself that his focus needed to be on the task force and on finding dangerous weapons smugglers and getting justice for Kenyon Graves's family, not on his past with Isabella Whitmore.

Liam glanced at Jack, then back to the wall of fallen heroes. "It's been a long day. Just needed to remember there's a reason for all of this."

Jack stood shoulder to shoulder with him, and silence settled between them.

Standing in front of this wall had to be a very different experience for Jack. Liam had never worked closely with any of the officers pictured before him, though he'd met a couple of them briefly while working on cases that overlapped.

The wall had to cut Jack in a deep place. These were his people, and a couple of them had been friends.

Liam's gaze slipped to the most recent photo. Kenyon Graves's official portrait was similar to the others. An American flag hung on the left, while the South Dakota flag was on the right. In the center was Detective Kenyon Graves. Beneath the traditional uniform peaked cap, Detective Graves had short dark hair in a typical cut. His blue eyes seemed alive, even in the photo. "Feels like he's watching us. Like he knows what's going on." He'd met the man a couple of times, when they'd crossed paths on a drug case, but the meetings had been short and all business.

Jack looked briefly at Liam before he returned his gaze to the wall. "Sort of." His voice was heavy. "He was a good guy. Fun to be around. Loved his kids. Losing his wife was hard on him." He turned away as though he couldn't look any longer. "I can't imagine how those kids are feeling. Their mom is gone. Their dad is gone now, too."

Liam couldn't look away from the eyes in the photo. It almost seemed like he could see the grief behind them and in the lines along Kenyon's forehead, even though he was smiling. How hard had it been to go to work every day knowing he was the only surviving parent to twin three-year-old boys? Had he questioned his decisions? Lived long enough after the blast to think of the boys? Had he had regrets?

Liam had spent time with the twins, Austin and Beacon, on several occasions. When Kenyon had died, his best friend Raina McCord had taken guardianship of the boys. Since her sister, PCPD Patrol Officer Trisha McCord was dating DGTF member and fellow PCPD Detective West Cole, the boys visited HQ often. It was one way Raina aimed to keep the memory of their father alive, by allowing them to be around people who had worked with and loved him. She wanted them to know the kind of hero that Kenyon had been.

It might be working too well. Beacon had begun to insist

that he'd seen his father looking in the window. West Cole, concerned for the twins' well-being, often took Kenyon's former partner, a beagle named Peanut, to visit with the twins, hoping it would ease their grief.

"We should get upstairs." Jack interrupted Liam's wandering thoughts. "I'm curious what Daniel has that required an in-person meeting." He passed Liam without looking back at the wall and headed for the elevator, a slight limp slowing his walk.

Liam took one more look at the photo before catching up with Jack. Sometimes he forgot how close Officer Jack Donadio had come to being on that wall himself. Because he'd been shot in the line of duty several months before, his role on the task force kept him at headquarters assisting their tech whiz, Cheyenne Chen. The two of them worked well together. More than once he'd wondered if those two were building a deeper relationship or if they simply bonded over the job.

As they stepped into the elevator, he shook off that thought. He had relationships on his mind today because of Isabella, who was in his office with Guthrie. Agent Givens had retrieved her purse, sketchbook and notebook, and Isabella was working on a sketch of her assailant's boots and of the glimpse she'd gotten of his arm. She'd insisted she didn't want company, that she'd rather be alone.

If he hadn't known her, he'd have assumed she was trying not to get in the way, but Isabella had always retreated when things were difficult. She preferred to process on her own than with others. It had been one of the few sticking points in their relationship. How often had he accused her of shutting him out?

Had that been the thing that had driven her away on the night before their wedding? Had he been too—

"Hey, Liam?" Jack snapped his fingers in front of Liam's nose. "Elevator stopped."

Liam jerked his head back. Sure enough, the elevator door stood open.

He offered the lamest excuse possible for zoning out. "Long day." His office was one of the first on the floor and, as they passed, he slowed to peek through the window in the door.

Guthrie was curled up on his bed in the corner, fast asleep after the adventure in the wildness.

Isabella sat at his desk, her head bent over a sketch pad, though the pencil she held wasn't moving. From this angle, it was tough to tell if she was thinking or if she'd fallen asleep at her work.

As much as he wanted to be angry with her, he couldn't muster the emotion. Instead, he felt concern for her safety and concern for her emotional state, like he would for any victim. She'd been through repeated trauma today. He should offer her a counselor. Maybe he'd have Jenna suggest it to her.

He should probably see one as well, because her reappearance had definitely churned up some old issues.

"Let's go." Jack poked him in the back, and Liam realized he'd stopped in the center of the hall. "You're out of it today, Barringer." He glanced into Liam's office as they passed. "Is that the woman the kidnapper tried to grab?"

"Yes. She's a sketch artist. She's drawing what she remembers. An investigator from the Park Service is coming to talk to her later and get her statement, and I'll sit in as well. I'm hoping to be assigned to the case since I was on scene." He didn't know why he didn't fess up about the true nature of his relationship with Isabella. Maybe it was too raw.

"Rough day for her. For both of you, really." Jack walked into the conference room ahead of Liam and took a seat beside Cheyenne Chen, who looked like her day had been as long as Liam's.

As Liam took his seat, two other DGTF members walked in.

Cheyenne pointed to a plate in the center of the table. "I needed to wind down when I got home, so I made my grandmother's gingersnap recipe. Have at it. I don't need to take them all back with me."

There was a murmur of gratitude around the table as everyone reached for a treat. Cheyenne was a gardener and a cook, and she was forever bringing in meals or snacks to share. They'd probably all gained ten pounds in the handful of months since the task force had come together.

Crunching into a cookie, Liam scanned the group around the table. A lot of things had happened personally for the task force in those months. PCPD Detective West Cole, who was partnered with Kenyon Graves's K-9, Peanut, had started a relationship with one of his colleagues, patrol officer Trisha McCord. Their chief fugitive tracker, Deputy US Marshal Gracie Fitzpatrick, had vanished into WITSEC with the man in her life, a protected witness. Deputy Zach Kelcey and his wife, who'd been separated up until recently, had reconciled. Fargo police officer Lucy Lopez was engaged to Micah Landon, a dog trainer whose troubled brother Nick had led the task force to a new lead in the gun smuggling case. Other team members were walking through struggles of their own as they juggled their personal lives, their day-to-day cases, and the demands of the task force.

Now he was facing his own personal battle.

The team had formed a family and had one another's backs. It was tough to remember what life had been like without them.

Special Agent Daniel Slater entered the room with Plains

City PD Captain Douglas Ross, and the team fell silent. An all-hands, in-person meeting meant big news. Maybe they'd finally caught a break.

Daniel wasted no time. Pressing a button on his laptop, he brought up a screen that displayed two photos. One was an unremarkable portrait taken from a driver's license. The other was of two men in front of the Plains City Pizzeria. Neither was new.

Liam and the rest of the DGTF had studied both photos often. Brandon Jones and his brother, Hal, were suspected of being the heads of the gun trafficking ring that spanned North and South Dakota. The two men were moving massive amounts of weapons through the states to other locations as yet unknown.

Hal seemed to be the smarter of the two. Brandon was arrogant, liked to flash his street cred, and acted like a celebrity, often taking photographs or bragging to the crew at lower levels in the ring.

There was nothing new here, so what was this about?

In a rare move, Daniel stepped aside and allowed someone else to take point.

Jenna Morrow stepped up. "You guys know these photos well, I'm sure. Daniel and I have been tracking these two and, yesterday, we got a break. We tracked Brandon Jones to a diner in North Dakota and were able to get our hands on their table before it was bussed. Our patience netted us some chewing gum and a few other items."

It seemed the entire team leaned forward for more. This might be getting interesting.

"Cheyenne called in some favors and fast-tracked DNA testing. Turns out Brandon and Hal Jones aren't actually Joneses. Their real names are Brandon and Hal *Murray*. Our dynamic duo have lengthy criminal records including—"

"Gunrunning?" West Cole cut in, and Daniel shot him a look. Their task force leader wasn't a fan of interruptions.

But nobody could fault West. He'd lost a close friend when Kenyon died, and he now worked with Kenyon's K-9 partner.

"Close." Jenna hit a button on the laptop, and the screen changed to digital copies of a rap sheet. "Illegal possession of a large number of stolen weapons. We're definitely headed in the right direction with these two."

"Do we have enough to bring them in?" Sheriff's Deputy Zach Kelcey spoke up this time.

Daniel resumed leadership of the meeting. "So far, what we have is largely circumstantial. We've got photos and testimony from Nick Landon, but we're going to need more. However..." He held up his hand. "Our operation may have gotten more complicated. Six months ago, the brothers moved to Fargo and started living lives aboveboard. Not even a parking ticket between them."

That was shortly before Kenyon and his informant had been killed in a bombing.

Putting the two things together painted an ominous picture.

The Murrays knew that law enforcement was on to them.

And that made them ten times more dangerous.

Why couldn't she go home? Isabella rubbed her hands up and down her bare arms, wishing for the sweater she kept in her car, which had likely been towed to an evidence garage. At least the attacker hadn't taken her tablet, sketch pad, and purse, though they were little comfort when she'd been sitting here alone for what felt like hours.

Liam had brought her to this place and left her with nothing but her thoughts.

Isabella swiveled in the chair at the desk in Liam's office.

She'd paced the room so many times, it was shocking there wasn't a path worn through the carpet.

Now she stared at her sketch pad, feeling off-kilter. Several pages were scattered across the wooden desktop. The scarred arms that victim one had seen. A twisted silver rope bracelet with polished stones that victim two had described.

On her sketch pad, drawn from her own memory, malevolent brown eyes stared at her, shadowed by a cap and barely visible over a surgical mask.

A shudder ran through her, and she flipped the pad over. Those eyes had been the hardest to recreate. As she'd sketched, she'd gone to that professional place where her emotions couldn't interfere, where her job was to listen to the witness, ask prompting questions, and sketch what she heard.

Today, she *was* the witness. Walking the tightrope between personal and professional, trying to distance herself from the memory while also engaging it, had left her weak. Now that she was looking at the finished sketches, her emotions burst forth.

Crossing her arms on the desk, she buried her face in the semidarkness. *God, it's too much. How can You expect one person to handle everything You're throwing at me? It's not fair. It's not—*

She tried to stop shivering. She was in relative safety in a police station in Plains City, South Dakota. She wasn't being assaulted in some unknown location, as she easily could have been.

Her body wasn't hidden in the wilderness.

She was alive and safe. For that, she should be thankful.

Still, she couldn't deny the tears that leaked out and ran down her forearms, damp and warm. She might be blessed, but she was also human.

She was a human whose life had nearly ended on a Badlands back road not once, but three times in the space of an hour.

Calista Franklin hadn't survived. Odds were high that Guthrie had alerted on the body of victim number three, Stephanie Parry, a twenty-seven-year-old physician's assistant who worked at Meadowlark Regional Hospital. She had disappeared after getting gas before a night shift in the ER.

Isabella had looked their killer in the eye.

The shudders drove her to her feet. She leaned forward, fists pressed against the desk, eyes locked on the sketch of scarred forearms. Those forearms had imprisoned her. Those hands had taken lives. Those—

A soft sound came from her right, then a warm weight pressed against her leg.

With a shuddering inhale, she looked down and met Guthrie's deep brown eyes that seemed to say he understood.

Sinking into the chair, Isabella cradled his face in her hands and rested her forehead against his. "You're a good guy to have around, aren't you, Guthrie?"

He let her sit with him until her bones stopped quaking and her mind stopped racing. When he sensed that she'd relaxed, he shook his head and loped back to his bed in the corner, where he curled into a giant ball of fur.

Guess she'd been comforted enough. "Thanks, Guthrie. I think." She smiled at the resting K-9. He was a working cadaver detection officer, not a therapy dog for a woman who'd had too much thrown at her for one day.

Isabella sat back in the chair and stared at the door, wrapping her arms around herself to ward off a chill she couldn't shake. She definitely should have asked for her sweater. She was two seconds from curling up beside Guthrie to keep warm.

She scanned the room, her gaze stopping on a wooden

armoire. The doors were opened slightly. Maybe Liam kept a coat in there.

There was a time when she'd have thought nothing of opening his closet to grab a jacket.

That time was long past.

She looked at the office door then back to the armoire. She couldn't.

Could she?

She was desperate and freezing. She could get warm and put his jacket back before he knew she'd borrowed it.

Another shiver urged her to the door, and she looked inside. The rail held a couple of empty coat hangers, but balled up on the floor was a sweatshirt he'd probably tossed inside.

Some things never changed. He'd always been the guy who had to pick his clothes up off of the floor when she visited his college dorm room. Most of the time, he'd tossed a pile onto the floor of his closet to deal with later.

She grabbed the sweatshirt and tugged it on, then went back to the chair. This was crossing a line, but desperate times called for desperate measures. It was only for a few minutes. No harm, no foul.

Except, as she sat back in the chair, the scent of him settled around her like a warm cloud. It was a blend of the same brand of soap he'd always used and something that was uniquely Liam.

This was a mistake, but she wasn't about to rectify it. For a minute, she'd be "that girl." She'd close her eyes and pretend everything had gone the way it should have. That she hadn't had to walk away from the man she'd intended to spend the rest of her life with. The man who had loved her well and had held her heart carefully in the palms of his hands.

Folding her arms on the desk, she rested her forehead on them and allowed the memories to form. The way the sunlight had fallen through the windows of the art history class she'd loved at Kansas University... It had illuminated the guy who'd merely endured the class because he'd thought it would be an easy elective.

He'd been wrong.

She'd been aware of his presence every time he walked into class, but she'd been careful not to let him know. She'd refused to be the girl who crushed on a guy in her very first semester.

Except that, in all of her not looking, she'd missed that he was noticing her as well.

At first, she'd thought it was random when she'd answered a question in class and he'd approached her afterward to ask for help with the course material. Much, much later, he'd confessed he'd been waiting for an opportunity to talk to her, and he'd finally approached her with the excuse of needing a tutor. They'd met once a week for almost a month before he asked her to grab lunch. Then he'd invited her to an art exhibit. Then he'd taken her to dinner, which in their broke college days had meant fast-food tacos.

To this day, those tacos were the most amazing meal she'd ever eaten. That was the first time their conversation had turned personal. They'd still been talking when the restaurant closed at two in the morning.

They'd been inseparable after that, building a friendship that layered feeling upon feeling until he showed up at her door the night before Christmas break. She'd been headed to apartment sit for a friend who was going home for the holidays, and Liam had already packed to head home to his family near Denver. He'd been flustered and nervous when he asked if she wanted to see the Christmas lights in a small town near campus.

That night had felt different. The air between them had

been charged as they'd walked dimly illuminated paths strung with thousands of lights and decorations. She'd thought she was dreaming when he hesitantly took her hand.

She'd been *convinced* she was dreaming when they stopped in a secluded area to look at a particularly tall Christmas tree and he'd kissed her. So awkward. So sweet.

He'd stolen her heart and had never given it back.

They'd been so young, but they'd grown together over the next three years. They'd made plans for the future. They'd seen each other through good and bad. They'd told each other everything.

Except the truth.

She'd kept silent about the one big part of her life that she couldn't share, not without dragging him into danger.

When that danger had come knocking on her door the night before their wedding, she'd had no choice but to walk away without telling him why. It had gutted her to pack a bag and flee, knowing she'd wounded him deep into his heart.

But her father and brother had given her no choice. They'd threatened Liam, and the criminal organization her father had run meant he could make good on those threats anytime. It was the reason she'd fled her family in the first place…but they'd found her that night and derailed her happily ever after.

A year ago, a massive sting operation had shut down her father's trafficking empire and landed several of her family members in federal prison, but that hadn't freed her. She'd hidden her family from Liam, and it had ripped them apart. There was no going back now. Her happily ever after was lost forever.

SEVEN

"Wait up." Jenna's voice bounced down the hallway.

Liam stopped outside of the break room with his hand on the door handle. Word was that Cheyenne had stocked the fridge with individual servings of homemade spaghetti that just needed to be reheated in the microwave.

She made excellent spaghetti. He'd planned to duck in, grab a couple of containers, then get out before anyone noticed. "In a hurry, Jenna." He twisted the doorknob and headed into the break room. He was starving, and Isabella probably was as well. It was also past Guthrie's dinnertime. In all of the chaos, he'd had little time to do more than give his partner a handful of treats to tide him over. "I need to eat. Guthrie needs to eat."

"And Isabella does, too." Jenna followed him into the room. She shut the door behind them, then stood in front of it with her feet planted wide and her arms crossed. Jenna had likely already eaten since she carried snacks with her everywhere she went—the woman was a walking vending machine.

Grabbing two plastic containers, Liam sighed, shut the door, and headed for the microwave. At the counter, he popped one open and was hit with the scent of tomatoes and spices before he even saw what was inside. Jenna was a shark, and she smelled blood in the water. She wasn't going to let this go.

He swung toward her. "You know, I had a conversation with you and Cheyenne in a weak moment when I let my guard down. It wasn't an invite into my past life. Ask me anything you want about the cases we're working, but any further discussion about Isabella is off the table."

"Because she still causes you pain." There was crunching as Jenna popped crackers from a packet into her mouth, but then her voice cleared. "You're not over what happened."

Enough was enough. "You think? How exactly does a guy get over it when the woman he loved for four years just… disappears? No explanation. No nothing. Oh yeah, and it's right as they're supposed to start their lives together. That's a pretty tough thing to brush aside, don't you think?" He snapped the words with all of the emotion that had been building since he'd realized the woman in distress was Isabella.

The microwave beeped, but he ignored it. Why was he taking food to Isabella anyway? She'd done nothing but rip his heart apart.

And yet she seemed so broken.

"I heard you asked to be put on her case. You need to think really hard about whether or not that's the right thing to do. I'm pretty sure if it got back to Daniel and your superiors, they would all give a big fat *no* when it comes to you spending one more second with Isabella Whitmore."

Jenna was probably right. Could he be objective? Could he set aside his questions and his pain and truly protect her while searching for a man who was terrorizing women who looked like Isabella? Whether he could or not, his gut twisted at the thought of handing her over to someone else who might not invest so much of themselves into protecting her.

What was wrong with him? He owed her nothing.

Yet, he'd once loved her. That meant something to him, even if it meant nothing to her.

Jenna looked into the plastic bag for more crackers, found none, and dumped the mess into the garbage before she dusted off her hands. "Look, the two of us have always been the cynical ones around here, at least when it comes to relationships."

That was true. The whole conversation with Jenna and Cheyenne about Isabella had started because none of them could fathom doing what former DGTF member, Deputy US Marshal Gracie Fitzpatrick, had done. After rescuing and subsequently falling in love with a protected witness, she'd left everything to go into WITSEC with him.

Jenna had said it seemed too fast. Liam had responded that love was an emotion that couldn't be trusted, and the ones you cared about most were the ones who would cut you the worst.

He still believed that, but he couldn't abandon Isabella. "I can't explain it, Jenna. I need to help her."

"You're softer than I gave you credit for." Jenna's smile took the punch out of her words. "I'm probably projecting my own issues onto you." Jenna had opened up to him about how her own love life had tanked after watching her mom ditch every man she dated growing up, including Jenna's dad.

"I'll be careful. I promise." He grabbed the containers from the microwave and hurried out before she could say anything more.

At his office door, he looked into the window, preparing himself for the sight of her yet again.

She was sitting at his desk, staring at her tablet. She'd twisted her hair up on the top of her head and anchored it with one of the pens from his desk. Wisps of blond hair drifted around her face, and strands hung on her neck where they'd escaped captivity. Her face was still streaked with dust but, otherwise, she looked exactly like she had so many times in the library or the coffee shop, bent over her books. The picture was exactly the same.

He leaned closer to the door. Um, yeah. It was *exactly the same* because she was wearing his sweatshirt.

This was too much. It was too familiar. She'd crossed a line, behaving as though nothing had happened and she was still entitled to his stuff.

No. This could not go on. Jenna had been right. He needed to turn Isabella over to someone else and let them deal with her.

She reached for her phone as he turned the door handle, and by the time he entered, she was standing.

"Isabella, this—"

"Liam." She rushed around the desk, clutching her phone, her expression strained. "It's my roommate. Someone tried to kill her."

"I promise. I'm really okay." Aiyana sat on the edge of the sofa, her feet planted on the floor and her hands clasped between her knees. Her dark ponytail fell over her shoulder as she watched Isabella pace the living room.

"I don't believe you." Isabella wrestled an overturned side chair to an upright position and sat, leaning toward her roommate and closest friend.

Other than a growing bruise on her cheek and red marks around her neck, she appeared to be unharmed. The killer had lunged from the darkness the moment Aiyana walked in the front door, striking a blow that knocked her to the ground before wrapping his hands around her neck.

Aiyana's training had helped her fight off her attacker, but he'd delivered another fist to her cheek, stunning her enough to allow him to race into the night.

Isabella looked around their shared living room. Other than the overturned chair and the coffee table lying on its side, the house was untouched. Whoever had come in hadn't been looking for a quick score in a robbery.

He'd been looking to kill.

Outside, red and blue lights silently rotated as multiple patrol vehicles blocked the street in front of their three-bedroom split-level. Like many of the houses in their neighborhood, theirs sat on a large sloping wooded lot. A walk-in basement at the rear had hidden Aiyana's attacker as he entered and made his way upstairs.

The camera they had mounted at the rear of the house had only picked up a shadowy figure, and the front doorbell camera had only caught a fleeing shadow. There was nothing solid to go on. All they had was a shapeless person in the shadows, awaiting Aiyana's arrival.

Isabella stood and walked to the front window. No, he hadn't been waiting for Aiyana. He'd been waiting for *her*.

She turned her back on the flashing lights and voices from outside and faced her roommate, who was staring at the floor. "I'm sorry. Whoever did this to you, he was looking for me."

"Girl, do not go apologizing to me." When Aiyana looked up, her face was a mask of professionalism. "You told me what had happened. You warned me he'd taken off in your car and had access to your license and registration, both of which contain our address. I'm the one who decided to come back here and pack a bag when I should have bunked at the department or with my parents. Or, I should have set up a sting to catch him if he showed up here." She stretched back and ran her fingers through her hair. "I didn't think he'd be gutsy enough to actually come to the house. According to everything I've read about the case, that's outside of his usual mode of operation."

"You're right." Liam followed his voice into the room from the stairwell. He'd gone downstairs with several members of Plains City PD to check out the point of entry, a window in the laundry room. "I had the chief up in Meadowlark brief me on the case on the drive over. Quite a bit of what's happening to Isabella is outside of this guy's usual scope. He's getting frenzied, escalated."

Aiyana stood slowly, her brows knitting together. It was tough to tell if she was skeptical of Liam or if she was in pain. "And you are?"

Liam held up his credentials then extended his hand. "FBI Special Agent Liam Barringer. I've been assigned to the serial kidnapper case."

Isabella inhaled sharply. "You...what?" Surely she'd heard him wrong. As far as she knew, Liam had driven her over here out of courtesy. Now he was here on official business?

That meant he would be working with her.

"I'm sorry." Aiyana held up a hand. "You said Liam Barringer?" She glanced at Isabella then back to Liam.

Liam didn't flinch. "I did."

Isabella dug her teeth into her tongue and tried her best to silently scream at her roommate. *Do not say you know who he is. Not a word.* Aiyana was direct and often lacked tact. If she smelled information, she went after it.

Now was not the time.

When Isabella had answered Aiyana's ad for a roommate three years earlier, the sound of the door to her future with Liam shutting behind her was still ringing in her ears. Her grief had been overwhelming, and she'd poured it all out to Aiyana on her first night in the house.

It was amazing the woman had let her move in.

Over the years, Isabella had spilled more to her roommate, including the real reason she'd had to walk away from Liam. Protecting his future and his life had cost her everything.

It had been Aiyana who had introduced the idea of her becoming a forensic sketch artist, and Isabella had fallen in love with the position. Not only did the job utilize her talents in a way that helped others find justice and closure, but it also gave her a sense of being a part of Liam's world. Law enforcement had always been his dream.

She'd walked away so that he could live it.

Aiyana knew it all. She was also likely to *say* it all.

Isabella held her breath and waited for the truth to pour out in a way she'd never intended for Liam to hear it.

Aiyana nodded slowly, looked Liam up and down, then clasped his hand. "Deputy Aiyana Macawi, Plains City PD." She dropped his hand but held his gaze. "So the FBI is involved? How did that happen?"

She knew the answer already, but the hint she'd dropped with her question was heavy in the air.

Liam didn't react. "Our unsub has kidnapped multiple women from Meadowlark, North Dakota, and he's crossed state lines into South Dakota. He released his first two victims, alive, in the Badlands. The third is still missing, although we expect an update on her status soon. The fourth was found dead, also in the Badlands, where Isabella was attacked. When he crossed state lines, he put himself on the federal government's radar."

"Mmm-hmm." Aiyana turned from Liam, dismissing him as though he was the one who had left Isabella at the altar and not the other way around. "I'm going downstairs to talk to Captain Morrison, and then we're all getting out of here. Pack a bag while you're here, Isabella. I'm sure Special Agent Barringer can arrange for a safe house, right?" She strode past Liam toward the stairs, pausing next to Isabella. "Pretty sure I've never seen that sweatshirt before. Is it new?" With a smile that said she knew exactly what she *wasn't* saying, Aiyana headed down the stairs, her bearing all business.

Forget the sweatshirt. Her friend was covering up her fear over an assault.

And she didn't want to go to a safe house. She'd lose herself if she was forced to sit still in hiding. She needed to be moving.

And the first place she needed to move was to help Aiyana.

Isabella moved to follow her, but Liam put a hand on her shoulder before pulling it away. "Let her go. If she has to be professional to get through this, then that's what she needs to do. I watched you do the same thing earlier."

He was right. There was no way Aiyana was going to spill her emotions for everyone to analyze, not now and not ever. Chances were high she'd never speak of this night again… except to interrogate Isabella about how Liam had come to be on the scene.

"She's right, though." Liam eyed her. "That's an interesting sweatshirt."

In all of the rushing and fear since Aiyana's call, she'd forgotten she was wearing it.

Embarrassment heated her skin, but she ignored it.

Tugging at the shirt's arms, she moved to pull it over her head. The house was chilly, and she'd probably shiver in her short-sleeved shirt, but that was beside the point. Her intention had been to put that sweatshirt away before Liam ever saw her in it, not to parade around in it for half of the night.

It was way too…

Well, it was way too everything.

Liam looked past her. "Don't worry about it. My office is

usually freezing. I should have offered you a jacket or something in the first place."

"Why?" She whirled toward him, and the haphazard bun she'd pulled her hair up in collapsed. His pencil hit the floor and her hair slipped to her shoulders. "Why are you being nice to me? I don't deserve this." His unmerited kindness was going to be her undoing.

Crossing his arms, Liam widened his stance. His gaze hardened. "No, you don't."

Isabella almost choked on her next breath. Well. That was definitely honest.

"Right now, Isabella, you're a victim. You're on my watch and in my care. Beyond that, believe me, there's no reason for me to be nice to you." His hazel eyes were impassive, his expression closed. "As far as I'm concerned, I met you this afternoon when a man tried to kidnap you. You're part of the job. Don't start thinking you're anything else."

His words cut more than she'd ever admit. He had no idea of the sacrifice she'd made for him, and she couldn't tell him now. As far as he knew, she'd callously walked away from him. He probably thought horrible, evil things about her.

But he didn't have to voice his apathy so plainly.

Stinging tears pierced the backs of her eyes and filtered into her nose. Turning away, she headed for the stairs. "I'm going to pack. And I'm going to clean up a little." She was dingy and dusty and sweaty, and she needed to cry in the shower like she had a thousand times before.

Otherwise, being with Liam Barringer would break her heart all over again.

EIGHT

He was an idiot.

He'd blame his emotional outburst at the house on the fact that it was one in the morning and he wasn't anywhere near getting to sleep tonight.

In the rear of the SUV, Guthrie snored softly, a sure sign that his partner was as exhausted as his human companions.

In the passenger seat, Isabella's head rested against the headrest with her eyes closed. Her arms were crossed on her stomach. Even in the darkness, the diamonds and sapphires on her right ring finger seemed to shine.

He wanted to ignore the sparkle, but it raised so many questions. Why hadn't she tucked it away somewhere? Sold it for cash? Did it actually mean something to her?

Why did he care?

It was too late and his walls were too unstable for him to consider any of those things now. Exhaustion led to mistakes he couldn't afford to make.

Isabella had been virtually silent since she'd grabbed a quick shower and packed her bags. She hadn't argued about going to a safe location or about riding with him. She hadn't said anything at all, had followed instructions and moved mechanically where she was told. Either she was too tired to function or she was done with him after what he'd said.

Ironic, really, that *she* was giving *him* the cold shoulder.

When she'd come downstairs, she'd draped his sweatshirt over a chair, not even bothering to hand it to him where he stood by the front door, keeping watch as Plains City officers and Pennington County deputies left the scene.

They'd been reluctant to leave a fellow deputy, and the last sheriff's department cruiser hadn't left until Aiyana had joined them. While they assumed the attacker had mistaken her for Isabella, they were being careful. Even so, she'd declined the offer of a safe house and would spend the night with a friend, while Liam and Isabella headed to an out-of-the-way motel that Daniel had secured. Jenna and Daniel would meet them there.

He checked his mirrors as he merged onto the highway, then looked over at Isabella. He never should have tipped his hand to her. He should have kept it strictly professional. Those few words he'd allowed himself had let her know she'd hurt him badly and that the pain was still fresh.

He gripped the steering wheel, the darkness and the late hour ripping through the barriers he'd carefully constructed around his heart. Flaming anger burned through.

She had no right to act like he was the problem. She hadn't been dressed to the hilt in a tux and ready to head to the church with his lifelong buddy Trei when the text came to say she was gone. She hadn't felt the ripping pain of reading a note that simply said *I'm sorry. You won't understand, but I have to go. I will always love you.*

She'd have to forgive him if he didn't believe that.

She hadn't been the one to realize she was the loser who'd believed in love but who'd been literally left at the altar. She hadn't had to live in the apartment they'd decorated together with the furniture they'd bought together.

She hadn't had to do anything except change her number

and block his emails. Isabella had tripped off into her new life like he'd never existed.

And now she had the audacity to act like *he'd* done *her* wrong.

"I'm sorry."

Liam jerked at the whisper.

Isabella hadn't moved. Maybe he'd imagined the words he'd always needed to hear from her.

But even as he convinced himself he was dreaming with his eyes open, she sat up, staring out the front window, her fingers knit together on her lap. "I shouldn't have grabbed your sweatshirt. It was cold, and—"

"*That's* what you're sorry for?" Enough was enough. "You left me. Worst of all, you left me with no reason why. You. Just. Left." He bit the words off and spat them out. "You ran over my life like a steamroller, left me bleeding, and all you're sorry for is that you wore my sweatshirt? Thanks. I was truly upset about that."

Her chin dropped to her chest.

For miles, the only sound was the thumping of his pulse in his ears. He wouldn't pity her. He wouldn't apologize for saying things he'd held in for years.

He had questions. So many questions.

He had pain. So much pain.

As he simmered in his anger, he tried to distract himself with his job. He watched the mirrors and the road ahead. At this time of night, few cars traveled between Plains City and the Badlands. It was a frequent tourist area, and most were already in bed, preparing for a day of exploring.

He drove the exact speed limit. Most cars would pass. If one hung back, then he'd know he'd picked up a tail. *So far, so good.*

At least things were good outside of the vehicle. Inside, a storm gathered.

Isabella clicked her tongue behind her teeth. When she spoke, her voice was controlled. "I meant that I'm sorry I hurt you. I never meant to bring up the past. I should have thought more about how borrowing your shirt would make you feel. It's a...metaphor for..." Her voice cracked. She cleared her throat and turned away to stare out the passenger window. Her fingers kneaded together, an action he recognized meant she was stressed or scared. "I can't give you an explanation. I had good reasons. Ones that you..." She sniffed. "I wish I could tell you, but I can't. I'm just sorry."

A pickup passed, and Liam watched it slip in front of him and continue on. In the rearview, two vehicles approached, one in his lane and one in the left lane. Neither set off alarm bells. He was free to focus on what he wanted to say. "You made the executive decision to call everything off. You left me to deal with the fallout, and you can't even give me a reason." He kept his voice low. Yelling would do no good. He wasn't that type of guy anyway. He'd never been one to shout in anger. He simply hadn't been raised that way.

Although some days, he wished he could stand on a peak in the Black Hills and shout his lungs hoarse. Maybe the pressure would release and he could heal. "You left me with no closure, Isabella. That might be the worst part."

"You don't have to do this. You can hand me over to another agent." The words fell like dead weight between them.

That was the part she'd never understand. Even he didn't grasp why, but he needed to be the one to work her case, the one to protect her.

God had a sense of humor. Maybe this was how he'd get the closure he needed in order to move on with his life.

Maybe he was the only one who could do the job. He glanced in the side-view mirror. Maybe—

The car on his left disappeared into his blind spot and stayed there.

Adrenaline hit his system. A quick look into the rearview showed the second vehicle still riding in his lane at the same distance as before.

But that car he could no longer see... It had kept a steady pace until it slipped in where he couldn't track it. The only way he knew it was still there was the headlights shining on the asphalt. He looked over his shoulder, barely able to see the car's hood.

In the back of the SUV, Guthrie picked up on Liam's agitation. His partner stood and walked to the small door between the front seats, whining softly.

Isabella turned away from the window to look at Guthrie then at Liam. "What's going on?"

"Nothing." There was no need to alarm her. "This car's taking its time passing us."

She leaned forward, trying to look across him. "Is that a problem? Do you think—"

"Sit back. And no." At least, he hoped not. If it was, he didn't need Isabella to make herself more visible if someone was trying to sight a weapon into his SUV. Nor did he need her to have her seat belt loose if the driver pulled a PIT maneuver and tried to spin them out.

Something that dramatic was unlikely with another car in the vicinity.

Unless that car was involved, too.

He checked again, and the second car remained in position, possibly a little farther back than before. It didn't appear to be a threat.

He held the steering wheel tighter, palms dampening and shoulders tensed, ready to turn into the spin if a blow came.

But the car stayed where it was, cruising in his blind spot.

He chewed the inside of his bottom lip. Maybe he should call Daniel. He shouldn't have made this run without backup, but Jenna and Daniel had gone ahead to secure the motel, and no one else had been free to escort them.

He'd have to handle this himself. Step one was to get a good look at whoever was driving that sedan. "I'm going to ease up on the gas and see if he pulls up alongside. If he does or he passes, then we'll know he's no threat." Sometimes, particularly when they were driving tired, people got distracted and simply zoned in on another vehicle, keeping pace with them in a drifting haze.

"And if he doesn't?" Isabella's voice was small.

"Then he'll know I'm on to him." Liam was locked tightly into professional mode, their personal issues secondary to what could be an imminent life-threatening assault.

Bracing himself, he eased up on the gas.

The car crept forward, pulling door-to-door with his SUV.

Guthrie whined.

Liam looked over with authority.

The gray sedan was packed with what looked to be high schoolers, singing animatedly with the radio. The driver had her cell phone in hand, the screen illuminating her face. Likely, in her distraction, she'd tagged onto his car and held position.

He was relieved and also furious. The texting and driving thing never failed to set him off. It was thoughtless and dangerous.

He tapped his horn for a short blast, then pressed his badge to the window.

Five faces turned toward him.

Horrified, the driver dropped her phone then slowed and fell in behind him, likely believing he was a local cop. She took the next exit, probably praying out loud that he wouldn't spin a U-turn and ticket her.

Good thing for her the FBI didn't deal in traffic violations.

Bad thing for everyone else on the road though. He prayed she'd learned her lesson and wouldn't hurt someone in the future.

Isabella sagged in her seat. "That was a little too much unnecessary drama."

"Yeah." The road ahead of them was dark. He glanced at her, then into the rearview.

The lights behind him had accelerated and were approaching quickly.

No one else was in sight.

Someone had picked their moment, and they were about to make the most of it.

Liam bore down on the gas, but the lights kept getting closer.

He swallowed an unfamiliar rush of fear. "Hang on. This isn't over."

No. It was just beginning.

Isabella grabbed the handle over the door. There was no way this was happening. "I thought you said we were fine."

"Somebody's been behind us for awhile, but they've kept their distance. I got distracted by our party-bus friends, and…" Liam looked at her, then into the rearview. On the steering wheel, his knuckles were almost white. "Now they're gaining fast."

At the door between their seats, Guthrie stood at attention, rocking gently with the SUV and watching Liam for his cues. What could the K-9 do other than plant his four feet and hold steady?

What could Isabella do other than pray?

Lord, I don't understand everything that's going on, but I know something is going on. Please make it stop. Please keep us safe. Please.

She really didn't have words, just racing emotions she knew He'd understand. The Bible said He did, so she had to believe. Nothing else made sense. Her *why* had no answer.

God could stop this, so why didn't He?

Lord, I—

"What's up, Liam?" A female's voice came through the speakers, putting an end to Isabella's scattered prayers.

Liam must have called someone.

"Cheyenne?" Liam's voice was tight. "Hang on. Isabella?" Reaching behind him with his right hand, he unlatched the door between them and the back seat. "You pet Guthrie. We're going to be okay."

Did he think Guthrie needed comforting or that she did? As Isabella slid the door open and reached inside, Guthrie nosed her hand onto his head. She slipped her fingers to the thick skin at his neck and kneaded it, feeling slightly better, but not much.

"What's going on?" The voice came again, less breezy this time. "Are you in trouble?"

Ahead of them, the dark highway stretched into infinity. Liam's attention bounced between the mirrors and the road. "Chey, I've got a tail." He gave their location. "Get whoever you can out here. I have a pretty good idea we're about to take down a killer."

"If he doesn't take us down first." Isabella couldn't help the words that trickled out.

"Thanks, Cheyenne." Liam ended the call by punching

a button on his steering wheel. "Nobody's taking us out as long as I'm driving."

Isabella swallowed hard, her fingers gliding along Guthrie's short fur. The K-9 licked her forearm and settled down with his chin on the headrest.

If only she could be as calm as Liam's partner.

Liam had always been confident, but his attitude now was downright cocky. It probably had to be in order for him to believe he could get them out of this situation alive.

He remained focused on his driving. "In a few seconds, I'm going to make a very abrupt, very high speed lane change. Be ready."

Tightening her grip on the handle above the door, she also wrapped her fingers around Guthrie's collar. How that was supposed to help, she had no idea, but it made her feel like she was doing something useful, possibly keeping the K-9 from being thrown around the rear compartment.

Liam lifted his foot from the gas and the SUV slowed. "Now!" He jerked the wheel to the left.

Tires squealed. The SUV rocked and felt as though it lifted off the ground, nearly rolling before it righted itself.

Liam slammed on the brakes.

Rubber scraped pavement.

Isabella screamed, although she didn't want to.

A dark car shot past them in the other lane.

The SUV shuddered and rocked back and forth several times before it stopped in a fog of tire smoke and burned rubber.

She was going to be sick. If the fear and the motion didn't get to her, the smell certainly would.

Guthrie was on his feet, his legs planted and his muzzle pointed straight ahead.

Isabella eyed him, searching for wounds or signs of distress, but the K-9 appeared to be fine, just on high alert.

Kind of like her...if she managed to keep her dinner.

The inside of the vehicle suddenly glowed with red light.

Muttering under his breath, Liam shoved the SUV into Reverse and roared backward up the highway.

Planting her feet and hanging on with a strength she never knew she had, Isabella fought to keep her back against the seat and stared out the front windshield.

A dark sedan had slammed on its brakes in front of them. It had no license plate and no bumper stickers or identifying marks. Other than the make and model, there was nothing distinct about it.

The car didn't move as Liam backed farther away then slammed on the brakes again a safe distance up the highway.

Isabella slammed against the headrest. She swallowed hard and gulped air, begging God for mercy for her swirling stomach and her spinning head. Begging Him for safety from this relentless assault.

After long moments where the only sound in the vehicle was the three of them breathing, the sedan suddenly gunned the engine and roared away with tires spinning. When it had gone about a tenth of a mile, the headlights and taillights vanished.

"He shut them off." Liam smacked the steering wheel, then eased the SUV to the side of the road.

"You're not going to follow him?" Her motion sickness forgotten in her ire, Isabella disentangled her hand from Guthrie's collar as she threw her right hand toward the fleeing vehicle. "He's going to get away. We can catch him. We can—"

"And do what?" Liam snapped. "I have no backup. Say he slams on the brakes and opens fire. Say he has an accomplice and lures us into a trap before help gets here. As much as I want to put an end to this, I'm not going to charge into the unknown when I have you in the vehicle with me. You've been through enough, and we've had too many close calls. This guy is escalating, and I don't like it. Clearly, he's fixated on you, and this is more dangerous than we thought."

Everything in her deflated as a chill wrapped around her. Her body, her mind, her heart…they all went numb.

Liam called Cheyenne and repeated their location and everything that had happened.

Ahead of them, in the opposite lane, several emergency vehicles appeared, lights flashing in the distance, racing closer.

She no longer cared. She no longer felt anything. All she wanted to do was sleep.

The same overwhelming emptiness had engulfed her on the night before her planned wedding, when she'd closed the door behind her father and brother and sank against it, sliding to the floor. That night, they'd demanded she convert her "FBI fiancé" into a patsy for their criminal organization. Refusal meant death for Liam. They couldn't risk her being married to a federal agent if he wasn't working for them as well.

So to protect Liam, she'd left him behind. Where she should have been overwhelmed by anger and grief at her family's vile demand, she'd felt nothing. The gulf that had opened in her heart was too expansive, and it seemed to swallow her whole.

It was the same now.

It had taken years for her to heal the last time, and part of her still felt like it lived in that abyss. The last thing she'd ever wanted was to feel so dead again, but she was overwhelmed and broken.

She'd lost herself, and the idea that this emptiness could be permanent terrified her more than any killer ever could.

NINE

Something was wrong with Isabella.

She'd not said a word in nearly two hours.

He leaned against the wall beside the door to her motel room and stared at the mountain that backed up to the older family-run business. The slope was a hulking shadow in the night that seemed to lie in wait to devour them.

It was far from comforting.

They were in the middle of nowhere near the Badlands, and the darkness was almost complete. When they'd arrived and gotten out of his SUV, the sky above had shone with stars on the moonless night, so dark that he'd been able to make out the Milky Way. At any other time, he'd have reveled in the sight. On this night, he'd given the sky a cursory glance before he secured the keys to the rooms Daniel had arranged for them and ushered Isabella to hers.

He'd left Guthrie with her, hoping the K-9 would offer some comfort and, although he was no guard dog, a bit of protection.

Maybe Guthrie's presence would break through the wall that had suddenly gone up around her. The silence was deafening, and it was impossible to tell if she was scared or angry or simply exhausted from the repeated attacks.

There was an option that was worse. He'd seen victims in

the past who had simply shut down. Their emotions couldn't handle the trauma and took them to a place that was either deep inside of themselves or far away in their minds in an attempt to hide from the fear. If she'd gone there, it might take a lot to get her back.

Not that it was any of his business. His job was to keep her alive and to bring a killer to justice before he could kill again or kidnap anyone else. It certainly wasn't to heal the woman who had taken a machete to his heart.

If that was the case, why did he care?

He balled his fists and pressed his knuckles into his thigh. It was too late to be thinking about any of this. Emotions couldn't be trusted after two in the morning. They were out of whack and uncontrollable...

And maybe too honest.

He shook off the disturbance that thought brought on and scanned the parking lot for hidden threats. Once he knew the area was secure, he desperately needed some rest.

Several cars dotted the small lot. His was parked behind the building out of sight from the two-lane road. Jenna and Daniel were parked near him and were currently walking the area with their partners.

When local law enforcement had arrived at their location on the highway, Liam had briefed them about what had happened and described the car. They'd put out a BOLO. The odds of them finding anything based on such scant intel were low.

Likely, the vehicle would be found ditched on the side of the road and wiped clean. The killer had been savvy enough to evade capture for months so, despite the errors he'd made in hunting Isabella, he was clearly smart enough to avoid detection. They had to hope the man's obsession would trip him up before he made a successful attack.

Pacing to the faded railing that lined the walkway, he braced his hands on the weathered wood and leaned forward to look at the sky. The stars seemed even brighter than they had earlier.

God, I don't know why any of this is happening. I don't know why You had me be the one to rescue Isabella, but I know You set all of that up and You had a reason. You don't have to show me, but I do need You to give me the strength to handle this. It's a lot more than I can carry, being around her, especially while she's in danger. You know how I feel, that I've never—

"Can't beat the sky out here, can you?" Daniel's footsteps were heavy on the outdoor carpet of the walkway. He stopped next to Liam, motioned for his Great Dane partner, Dakota, to settle at his feet, then leaned against the railing. Turning his head toward the sky, he followed Liam's gaze.

For awhile, neither of them spoke.

Liam was grateful for both the company and the silence. There was no doubt Daniel wanted an update, but there was also no doubt that Daniel would wait quietly all night if it took that long for Liam to feel ready to speak.

Considering how exhausted they all were and the ridiculously late hour, they didn't have all night. His defenses were low and his filter was nonexistent at this point anyway. "What do you want to know?"

"Whatever you want to share." Daniel didn't look away from the stars. "I get the feeling that Isabella Whitmore is not simply a victim you met for the first time today. You're a good FBI agent and you care about people, but you've been particularly on edge about her case."

Daniel was quietly perceptive. He watched. He studied. He came to reasoned and well-thought conclusions. There was no hiding from him.

It was annoying.

Liam looked at his team leader's profile and considered the man's quiet kindness. Okay, maybe it was annoying, but it was also kind of...comforting?

Boy, did he need some sleep.

Still, he might as well get this over with. Daniel was going to find out eventually. "Isabella Whitmore and I have known each other since we were freshmen in college. We were engaged. Three years ago, on what should have been our wedding day, she..." Liam flung his arms over the railing as though he was tossing away garbage. "No explanation. No contact. Today was the first time I've seen her since I told her goodbye one night believing I was going to watch her walk down the aisle toward me the next day." They'd had it all planned. Because Isabella's parents were gone, she was going to walk down the aisle on the arm of her favorite art professor, whose family had treated her like a daughter.

She hadn't given Dr. Davenport and his wife any reasons either. She'd simply disappeared.

Daniel's jaw tightened. Sudden tension poured off of him as though he was being pulled in every direction.

Liam let go of the railing and faced Daniel. Something was going on, and it had nothing to do with Isabella or the trafficking case.

Liam had beaten his own problems to death today. His gut said Daniel was battling something personal as well. "I don't really want to talk about it right now. Cheyenne knows. Jenna has been hounding me about it since she looked down in that stinking hole in the ground earlier and figured out who Isabella was." He studied Daniel, who didn't react. "What's going on with you? Is something wrong with Joy?"

He felt an immediate stab in his heart. Here he was worried about his own history, when Daniel was wrestling with a history he'd never known existed. A few months earlier, someone had abandoned a toddler at HQ. The child had a partially redacted birth certificate and a note that claimed she was related to Daniel. Further digging had indicated the little girl was born to a Serena Rogers, a woman Daniel had never met nor heard of.

Come to think of it, Daniel had said earlier that he was going to meet with a friend of his late father's. Maybe that meeting had been about Joy and Serena. "You learned something about Joy's mother, didn't you?" But why would Liam's story about Isabella have caused Daniel pain?

"This is about your problem, not mine." Daniel's voice was deep and a little ragged.

"Maybe not." Liam leaned his hip against the rail and crossed his arms, trying to look at ease when every muscle was on high alert. "I'm talked out. I think it's your turn."

"I'm not a talker, Liam."

"All the more reason to speak, *Daniel*." The task force leader never allowed them to hide things for long, and Liam was about to return the favor. "Let's hear it."

Daniel tensed as though he was either going to walk away or give Liam the berating of his life, but then his shoulders slumped. He stared at the sky for a long time before he spoke. "I will never understand why God does things the way He does. I mean, Joy is so…she's so much I didn't know I needed in my life. She's an amazing little kid. But how she was born is so…" He held up a hand without looking at Liam. "That's a deeper discussion for another day." He exhaled loudly. "I got a call on the way here."

"About Joy?"

"About Serena Rogers." Turning his back on the parking lot, Daniel crossed his arms. "I met with an old friend of my late dad's this evening after our team meeting, and he told me he was clueless. I guess his conscience started eating at him though, and…" Dragging his hand through his hair, Daniel glanced at Liam then stared at Isabella's door. "My dad had an affair when I was a kid."

"Dude." The gut punch was real. Daniel's father had passed away several years earlier. He'd talked often about how much he looked up to the man and how special their relationship had been. To learn something like that at a time like this? To know there had been such a deep betrayal of their family and that there would never be solid answers about why? That had to be…*wow*.

"I know. It's a lot." Daniel twisted his mouth and shook his head, clearly still working through the news. "Apparently, Serena was born out of that relationship. I have a half sister."

"And you're sure it's true? You never thought your dad would be the type of guy who would—" How did you even say something like that out loud?

"If it had come from anyone else's mouth, I wouldn't have believed it. The thing is, he has proof." There went the hand through Daniel's hair again, proof he was distressed. "Serena's mother wrote to my father and told him about his… about…well, about Serena."

Maybe it wasn't true. "There have been times when people fabricated a story about paternity in order to get something out of it. Maybe—"

"Dad wrote back, and his friend has both letters. Dad gave them to him for safekeeping, which is weird. You'd think he would have destroyed them or something." Turning back toward the parking lot, Daniel braced his hands wide on the railing and stared at the mountain behind the motel. "I can't believe what he wrote. My dad, who was such a great father, who was everything I could have asked for in a role model… He shut her down. Told her he wanted nothing to do with 'a child' and nothing to do with her either. He cut her off and made threats if she reached out again." He chuckled bitterly. "I haven't seen the letters yet, but he read them to me. He's sending me scans in my email. I'm not even sure I want to look at them."

How could he possibly respond to a situation like this? His own pain had been so deep when Isabella left, but she hadn't betrayed him the way Daniel was talking about, at least not as far as he knew. "Man, I'm sorry. I don't even know what to say."

"There's nothing to say, and I'm done talking about it." Releasing the railing, Daniel pulled his phone from his pocket and glanced at a text that lit the screen. "This is Cheyenne, so let's get back to your thing. She has DNA results from Isabella's vehicle and—" He squinted and looked closer at the text before he leveled a concerned gaze on Liam. "I hate to say this, but we've got bigger problems than we initially thought."

"Well, Guthrie, I know you're not a therapy dog, but you're definitely good company." Isabella sat on the floor in a small hotel room, her back against the bed farthest from the door that Liam had walked out of nearly an hour earlier.

He'd walked out and left her alone. How was that for irony?

Guthrie lay beside her in a big ball of dog, his back pressed against her hip. She'd rested her palm on his side for who knew how long, feeling the sleeping K-9 breathe. The warmth of his side rising and falling in a steady rhythm eased the fear she'd succumbed to in the car.

The affection she felt for Liam's K-9 partner broke through the numbness. Maybe she wasn't going to turn into an emotionless robot, moving through her days with a checklist in hand to know she was still alive. Maybe she was going to be okay.

First, she had to survive this onslaught. If this killer kept coming after her, sooner or later he was going to succeed.

She stroked Guthrie's floppy, silky ear with one hand, while the other rested on the cross tucked beneath her shirt. Liam had given it to her on the day she was baptized, and she'd never taken it off. He'd been by her side that day, so excited and supportive.

He was by her side now, too, which meant the killer might destroy Liam in his attempt to reach her.

She was definitely feeling again, because the thought of Liam taking a bullet stole her breath. She'd walked away from him, but she'd known he still lived and breathed and pursued his dream of making a difference in the world as an FBI agent.

She had not been above a little social media stalking on occasion to ensure he was still safe.

But the alternative was terrifying. If he stopped breathing... If he vanished from this world...

The pain in her heart was not in her imagination. It was very real.

Maybe she should disappear. Surely Aiyana would help her. Except she no longer had her cell phone. It was too easy to track. And, since all of her numbers were in the device, she had no idea how to call Aiyana without it.

Unless she wanted to trek across—

The door flew open and Isabella jumped up, fear ripping through her.

Guthrie scrambled to his feet and moved in front of her. Though he was no guard dog, he seemed to understand that Liam wanted her to be safe.

Liam. It took a few seconds for her brain to catch. It was him striding into the room.

He gripped his phone as though he wanted to crush it, and he never looked away from her as he slammed the door, questions and pain in his eyes.

"Liam?" His demeanor skipped lightning through her stomach. "Do we have to leave?" Surely whoever had tried to grab her wasn't in the area. How did that man know where she was at every turn?

Liam pressed three fingers against his forehead and closed his eyes as though his brain was trying to force its way through his skull.

Panic pushed against her skin, growing with every moment of silence. Her throat was so tight that she couldn't speak. Had someone died?

"Explain yourself." Liam drew in a deep breath and held it, then dropped his hand from his head. He tilted his chin up to imprison her in a gaze so strong she would never be able to break free. "Tell me the truth. For once." He held the phone out, the screen glowing.

What did he think she'd done? Isabella looked down at Guthrie as though he had an answer, but the K-9 walked to his partner and sat at Liam's feet, alert for a command.

Traitor.

On weak knees, she closed the gap and took the phone with shaking hands. She didn't even have to read it. One name jumped out and grabbed her by the throat.

She sank to the edge of the bed, unable to look away from stark black letters on the bright white screen. *Christian O'Leary.*

She couldn't look at Liam. Even if she'd wanted to speak, that pressure in her throat and the desert in her mouth made words impossible.

"Who are you?" Liam's voice was low, but it shook with a storm of emotions. If he'd connected that name to her, then he was feeling a lot of things, from anger to betrayal and maybe even fear.

She tried to read the screen, to see what sort of digital document he'd handed her, but her eyes remained locked on the name. She might be sick. She might die. She might—

"Isabella, those are the results of DNA testing done on *your* vehicle today. It picks up sweat, sneezes, everything. There were three main people whose DNA came back from your SUV." He stepped back as though she might attack him. "One was a match to the killer in the other cases. One was your roommate, who is in the system as a law enforcement officer." He took two deep breaths as though he needed to fortify himself. "The third is a familial match to Christian O'Leary."

She forced herself to look at Liam. He stared at her with the same anger and confusion as when he'd walked into the room. It was clear he was holding back things he wanted to say, maybe even to shout, but Liam wasn't the type to explode.

He pointed at her, his hand shaking slightly. "Either you are the only individual in existence who has no DNA whatsoever, or you're a member of the O'Leary crime family."

The ice-cold truth burned.

She could argue that DNA wasn't an exact science. It could be wrong, especially where familial matches were concerned.

But arguing would be pointless.

Weariness soaked in until it felt as though her bones turned into jelly. She was tired of hiding. Tired of keeping Liam in the dark and forcing him to question every beautiful thing they'd shared.

She held his phone out and looked away as he took it. It was time for the truth, and she spoke it in dead cold facts. "The name I was born with, is Isabella O'Leary. When I was sixteen, I emancipated from my parents, and I took my grandmother's maiden name. I graduated high school early, left Savannah for a random town that I found on a map of Kansas, and I never looked back."

"You told me you were an orphan."

"I was, in a manner of speaking." When she'd walked away, her parents had been furious and had told her not to come back. They had always demanded blind, unquestioning loyalty. Without it, their deeds were at risk of exposure.

Her parents and older brother had been shocked by her decision to walk away from the money and power that came with being an O'Leary. They'd expected her to follow in their footsteps, but she'd learned something different at the private school they'd deemed socially acceptable. Something that had gone over her brother's head.

She'd learned about right and wrong, about Jesus and his sacrifice. As she'd grown, she'd discovered that the life her family led was a life she didn't want. She'd made the choice to live in a way that didn't involve criminal activity, and she'd worked hard to stand on her own in a way that made God and herself proud.

She'd never feared they would harm her, because Christian O'Leary loved her in his own twisted way and had always hoped she'd return, but that protection didn't extend to Liam.

A federal investigation had left their organization in ruins, and many members of her family were in prison. She'd been questioned but not investigated, having broken ties with the family years earlier. She was a free woman.

Except she wasn't.

Although she was free of the O'Learys, she'd still lost the

man she'd loved. She could never go back and undo the pain she'd caused him by hiding the truth.

"I can't believe this." Liam dropped his hands to his sides and walked to the door. "You never trusted me enough to tell me the truth." He addressed the door, icicles hanging from every word.

He didn't understand. He'd never understand, but he deserved the truth, and now that it was in the open, she could speak it. "At what point was that supposed to be a conversation? On our first date over tacos? 'By the way, my family runs a shipping company that deals in a whole lot of questionable stuff and that has put them on the radar of the FBI and maybe even Interpol but nobody's been able to prosecute them because people disappear when they get too talkative and everyone who works for them is terrified. I don't have anything to do with them, but hey, you understand, right? Can you pass the salsa?'"

He scoffed and shoved his hands into his pockets.

Although he was correct that she'd hidden a huge secret from him, he had no idea what it was like to be in her position. He had two parents who loved him, one a nurse practitioner and the other a resort manager. Nobody looked sideways at him, wondering if he was going to become the next Al Capone. Nobody talked in whispers behind his back or refused to let their kids visit his house. Never once had he suspected that one of his school friends might be an undercover agent trying to get dirt on his family.

He hadn't opened the door on the night before his wedding to find his father and older brother standing there after nearly a decade of separation.

How many nights had she awakened with her father's deep Southern drawl crawling down her spine? *Izzy-girl, you're in the perfect position to protect your family. You have an*

FBI agent in your hip pocket. You can get him to do whatever you want. He's an asset to us. A protection. And if he refuses? Then he's a liability. You don't' want to know how I feel about liabilities.

She had strong suspicions about how her father felt about *liabilities*.

"I'd have understood." Some of the ice in Liam's voice melted as he turned to look at her, but the chill in his gaze lingered. "We'd have figured it out."

"It would have destroyed us." He had no clue that death had been on the table for them both. The truth was broken and choked. She sniffed at the dammed-up tears that stung her eyes and nose. "I couldn't let that happen."

"So you chose to destroy us on your own? Without my input?" He put one foot in front of the other as though he wanted to be closer to her, but his step faltered. "Is that why you walked away? Why you—"

The room went dark.

Isabella rocketed to her feet. "Liam?" She couldn't see anything. The inky blackness was complete.

There was a rustling sound, and it seemed Liam was approaching the door. "The entire property is out. Go get in the bath tub. Don't leave the room. Hopefully it's nothing. I'll be right here."

There was a soft click, the unmistakable sound of a pistol being drawn from a holster.

This was no outage. No mistake.

This was death, taking aim for one more shot.

TEN

When the bathroom door closed, Liam crouched low and curled around his phone, holding it near his chest as he swiped his thumb across the screen. In the total darkness, even dim light would shine like a beacon if it escaped around the edges of the curtains.

Daniel and Jenna had both sent texts.

Jenna and Augie were headed to the manager's apartment to see what they could learn.

Daniel was on the walkway outside, standing guard. *Holding off on calling local law enforcement. Don't want to tip our hand that we're here if this is nothing.*

None of them believed it was *nothing*. There was no such thing as coincidence. For the power to suddenly cut out in clear weather while a killer was stalking Isabella? Yeah, everything about this felt planned.

Gripping his phone in one hand and his Sig in the other, Liam straightened and pressed the phone against his thigh to hide the screen that would light up with incoming texts. He was dying to peek out of the curtains, but any movement could tip off the bad guy. At this time of night, most of the other lodgers in the hotel were asleep, and few would emerge to ask questions. If any did, Daniel would urge them inside to safety.

The bathroom door scraped softly. "Liam?" Isabella's low voice indicated that she hadn't obeyed his command to lie low in the bathtub. If someone opened fire, it was the safest place to be.

Although their unsub had shown no indication of using firearms, Liam still felt safer with her in the most secure place possible. "Take cover in the tub."

"Shouldn't *you* take cover?" Her whisper sounded like a shout in the stillness.

Dropping his head against the door, he stared in the direction of the dark ceiling. His eyes had adjusted enough to make out vague shapes, but out here there were no streetlights to soften the darkness. There were only the stars on this moonless night, and they weren't enough to bring detail into the room. "No, I shouldn't. Shut the door and do what I said until I tell you to come out."

It was several seconds before the door clicked shut.

Liam dipped his chin, but he rested his head against the door. In the darkness and with his mind still reeling from the revelations of the past half hour, leaning against something solid was staving off a strange sort of vertigo.

Isabella was the daughter of Christian O'Leary, a notorious transporter for traffickers of all stripes. He was in federal prison for operating as a shipping go-to for everything from guns to people. It had taken years for the FBI to bring that organization to justice. Associates either didn't speak, or they died before they could.

And he'd been engaged to Christian O'Leary's daughter. Nothing in the world could have shocked him as much as that information.

Why hadn't she been willing to tell—

His phone buzzed. Daniel. *Got motion at the rear of the*

parking lot. Checking it out. Jenna, update? Liam, step out on guard.

He gave the message a thumbs-up and pocketed the phone. As loathe as he was to leave Isabella alone, he had to obey Daniel's order. It was important that they knew where one another was at all times.

Besides, he'd be right outside the door.

He felt for Guthrie's head and rested his hand between his partner's ears. "Stay. Guard." While Guthrie wasn't specifically trained in protection, he would alert if anything got his attention. When Liam slipped out the door, Guthrie didn't move. His partner was—

Blinding pain shot through his cheek as a blow whipped his head to the side. He stumbled sideways, and his gun clattered to the concrete walkway. He threw his hand up to ward off another strike. What—

Something thin and heavy cracked against his wrist as his unseen assailant came at him again.

He was ready this time.

Liam threw his hand forward and knocked the blow toward the railing as he righted himself, facing off against a shadowy figure. Looking at his cell phone had destroyed his night vision. Hopefully his eyes would adjust quickly.

Behind him, the door slammed shut automatically. It would lock on its own, preventing his attacker from getting to Isabella...unless the man incapacitated him and was able to get to the key in his pocket.

"Daniel! Jenna!" He called for help as he widened his stance and prepared to fight.

The figure was merely a shape in the darkness. He wore bulky jeans and a heavy, shapeless sweatshirt pulled up over his hair. His face was shadowed, likely covered by a mask.

It was impossible to make out features.

He held what appeared to be a golf club. Thankfully, only the shaft had struck Liam, or the consequences could have been much worse than the bruise throbbing in his cheek.

Liam squared off. "FBI. Drop your weapon!"

Several doors opened along the walkway and people stepped out, roused by his shouts and groggily asking questions.

The shadow froze. After a heartbeat, he sprinted to the right, racing for the stairs at the far end of the walkway, shoving people out of the way as he ran.

Liam couldn't leave his weapon behind. He felt for his gun, scooped it up, and moved to pursue. "Get back inside!" He commanded the bystanders to get to safety, but in their sleepy confusion, they didn't seem to understand what he was ordering them to do.

He couldn't give chase and leave Isabella unprotected. He couldn't fire at a fleeing suspect, even if there weren't civilians in the way. He could only holster his sidearm and call Daniel.

"Heard you yell. On the way." Daniel was clearly on the run. "Jenna's coming with Augie."

Hopefully, Augie could pick up a scent and track the guy. "Suspect took off toward the main road on foot. I've got civilians in the way." He stared helplessly in the direction the perpetrator had fled, his chance to end this thing vanishing into the night.

Again.

"Stay with Isabella. Jenna and I are on it." Daniel ended the call.

His eyes adjusting to the darkness, Liam could make out probably half a dozen people milling around on the walkway. "Go inside. There's nothing to see here." The suspect had fled, so it was likely none of them were in danger.

Grumbling, most obeyed.

Pulling the key from his pocket, Liam felt for the doorknob and entered the room. Once inside, he turned on his phone's flashlight and scanned the space. There was no way anyone had slipped past him, but thick darkness drove him to be sure no monsters lurked in the shadows. With Guthrie at his heels, he crossed the room by the light from his phone and knocked twice on the bathroom door. "It's Liam. He's gone."

The door swung open, and Isabella stood in front of him, illuminated by the light he'd aimed at the floor to keep from blinding her. Though she was dressed simply in jeans and a gray T-shirt, she looked ethereal in the semidarkness, like something out of the dreams he'd had with varying frequency over the years. Each time, he'd awakened only when he'd reached for her and she vanished into mist as his fingers touched her.

Exhaustion and adrenaline lent a surreal quality to the moment, twisting his thoughts and leaving his heart without its usual guardrails. Their history kept slipping through the cracks, and he couldn't fight it back.

"You nearly killed me." The words sliced his throat on the way out, but he couldn't stop them. This entire situation was so messed up, so twisted into knots and so utterly outside of reality that he couldn't control his thinking anymore. Here he was, confessing the things he'd sworn he'd never say to her. Letting her know that she'd wounded him deeply when she'd disappeared.

"I know, and I never meant for that to be the case." The tears in her eyes glistened in the dim light. "Nothing happened the way that I wanted it to. Liam, you have to know I never wanted to walk away from you, and if I'd had a choice, I never would have done so without talking to you."

He shook his head, her words the hammer and nails that

rebuilt the walls she'd torn down. "There is always a choice, Isabella."

She didn't show any outward sign that she'd heard him. She simply let tears run unchecked down her cheeks.

It was impossible to look away from her.

What had happened to make her walk away without talking to him? There had to have been a good reason. Had it caused her pain as well?

Did the fact that she still wore his ring mean that he'd never stopped holding a place in her heart?

Although his mind screamed that she should have come to him three years ago, his heart said that she must have felt a need to handle things the way she had. "What happened? Why would you just leave?"

She knit her fingers together and stared down at them, apparently trying to compose her thoughts.

Outside, his teammates searched for a killer. In here, the situation was no less dangerous.

He found himself tugged toward her once again.

Did he dare give in? Did she want him to?

She'd crushed him once before, and it had nearly killed him. The pain still cut. The dreams still haunted. The grief was still real. No matter what explanation she gave, it didn't change the fact that she'd chosen not to talk to him. That she'd decided, on her own, to pour gasoline on their future and set it on fire.

"It doesn't matter." He stepped back, putting space between them so he could breathe air not heavy with the scent of her. Something both spicy and flowery, different than before but something that drew him in.

She didn't look up when he spoke.

He took another step back. "The bottom line is that you didn't trust me. I can't forget that. We were supposed to go through life together, to share everything, to have each other's backs, and you couldn't stand by that. You couldn't keep your promise." That was the worst part. It wasn't that she'd left. If she'd tried to talk to him and they couldn't have come up with a solution together, things would have been very different. "I'll be here until we catch this guy or the FBI tells me I'm done, but beyond that?"

He turned away before his heart could betray him.

Beyond that, while he was protecting her, he had to be sure to protect himself.

She'd never been more exhausted in her life.

Isabella cradled the paper cup of cheap coffee that Jenna had brought from the hotel's small lobby before they'd rolled out to head back to the crime scene, where Guthrie had alerted on a potential grave site the day before.

As the miles passed beneath the wheels of Jenna's SUV, Isabella stared out the window at the sunrise that had pinked the sky with a riot of colors only a few minutes earlier. The day was now settling into the kind of blue-white heat that made both man and beast miserable.

After a night where she'd finally fallen into fitful sleep only a couple of hours before Jenna had awakened her, the heat promised to make her pounding headache and bad attitude even worse.

Liam had disappeared the night before, shortly after Jenna had arrived with Augie, who had attempted to track the suspect. It seemed he had a car waiting up the road, because there had been no scent to track.

Jenna had tossed and turned in a restless sleep after confessing she was frustrated at the killer's escape.

Isabella had spent the night staring at the dark ceiling, her mind a collage of shifting images. The kidnapper's scars.

The walls of the crevice. The approaching headlights in the darkness. The look on Liam's face in the dim light as he turned away.

She didn't know whether to pity him or punch him. He kept saying she didn't trust him, that she'd had a choice.

But what choice had she had? He wasn't the kind of man who would have let what her family had done simply slide by. He'd have chosen confrontation. He'd have chosen to fight the legal battle with them. He'd have asked what she knew and if she could help take them down, the exact same things they'd asked of her when it came to Liam.

Her father was a horrible man, but he believed in family, and he'd have never physically harmed her. But targeting Liam… that was another story. Cutting ties with him, severing what her family considered to be her influence over him, had been the only way to keep her father from hurting Liam.

Would he have believed her had she told him that, while she knew her family was into a thousand horrible things, there was nothing she could hand to law enforcement to prove it? That if she'd had hard evidence, she'd have already passed it along? Did he think she was the kind of person who would protect criminals, even if they were her flesh and blood?

"What made you want to ride out here today?" Jenna's question stopped her runaway thoughts. "I'd think the last thing you'd want to do is come back to the scene of the crime where we might be unearthing a victim."

How could she explain? Daniel had appeared earlier that morning and offered to escort her back to their headquarters in Plains City, but the very idea made her feel like she was quitting. She needed to come back. Needed to confront this nightmare place so it wouldn't haunt her forever. Needed to honor Stephanie Parry's memory if the woman truly had been buried out here alone. On the practical side, she also hoped that returning to the scene would bring back some more memories, more details she could add to her sketches and perhaps bring this man to justice more quickly.

She took a sip of coffee and tried not to make a face at the bitterness on her tongue. "What made *you* want to ride out here?" She might as well answer a question with a question. After all, Jenna wasn't assigned to the serial kidnapper case, yet here she was.

"I'm doing a favor for Liam. He and Guthrie are working the scene. I also thought you might want some company, and I think I was right about that. I'll be moving on as soon as we're done here. Daniel and I are heading out of town to follow up on a lead."

Isabella stared out the window, watching the stark scenery pass by. Well, that meant she'd have to ride to whatever her next secure location might be with Liam. It wasn't something she looked forward to. It seemed like every interaction between them deteriorated even more than she'd imagined it could.

"If I opened a dictionary, and I looked up the word *tortured*, I'm pretty sure I'd see a picture of your face right now." Jenna didn't look away from the road in front of her as she turned off onto the gravel road to the camping area, pausing only to roll down her window and show her badge to the park ranger standing guard.

Once they'd been waved through and the window was up again, Isabella looked away from Jenna. Her body recoiled at the thought of being here, of seeing the place where her life had very nearly ended not many hours before. Maybe if she fell back on fear, Jenna wouldn't figure out what was really digging lines into her face. "It's tough to come back here."

"Hmm." Reaching over, Jenna popped the center console

open and passed Isabella a granola bar. "It's not healthy, but I prefer chocolate chips over nutrition any day."

Confused, Isabella slowly took the bar and stared at the wrapper. While she couldn't recall the last time she'd eaten, she didn't remember asking for food.

"When I'm messed up in my heart and head, sometimes it's because my sugar's dropped too low. Just offering a way for you to bounce yours up again." Jenna shut the console. "If, in fact, the problem is something as simple as blood sugar. I'm assuming, since you're riding to the site with me and not with Liam, your silence might be a little more than a granola bar can fix."

Too many gut punches, too many threats, and too little sleep made the words wrap around Isabella like barbed wire. She dropped the granola bar into the cupholder. "Are you always like this?"

"Am I always freely sharing what I have with others? Yes. I am definitely a giver like that." Jenna's eyebrow arched, though she kept her eyes on the road. "Look, life is short, and if I can help then I don't need to stand on formality before I step in. You, Isabella Whitmore, clearly need help. You can bite my head off if you want, but that granola bar will taste a lot better."

Okay, so maybe she was a little cranky.

Isabella looked at the granola bar. It was the first thing in an entire day that didn't make her stomach feel like it was going to tuck tail and run.

Cautiously, she grabbed the bar, tore open the wrapper, and took a small bite.

It really was a chocolate wonder. In three bites, her makeshift breakfast was finished, and she pocketed the wrapper. They were nearing the crime scene, but the silence in the

SUV was too heavy to let it sit for even thirty more seconds. "What's Augie's specialty?"

In the rear of the vehicle, the German shepherd lifted his head at the sound of his name, looking between Isabella and Jenna. He lowered his head to his paws once he decided that no command was forthcoming.

"Augie is trained for suspect apprehension and he also does a little bit of scent work. Mostly, he's just a really good partner to have around." Jenna looked in the rearview, presumably at the K-9, then cut her eyes to Isabella with a veiled smile that was more of a silent *I saw what you did there*.

Yes. She'd diverted the conversation.

Now that she had food in her stomach, and the caffeine from the coffee was kicking in, maybe she'd been a little too hard on Jenna earlier. "Sorry I snapped. I haven't even talked to my best friend yet. When it comes to Liam..." How did she even begin to explain?

"Things are complicated?" Jenna pulled to the side of the road behind Liam's SUV and shut off the engine. "I know you guys used to be together, but I also know this... Love is complicated. It's hard to find. Might even be harder to keep. I definitely don't have the expertise to give you any advice, and I don't know your story, but I do know it's hard." She shrugged. "That's my two cents' worth of observation, whatever it's good for." She shoved the door open and got out.

Isabella didn't move as Jenna shut the door and then helped Augie out of the back. Jenna was right. Love was hard to find and harder to keep, especially when the secrets you hid to protect the man you loved ripped him away forever.

ELEVEN

Liam opened the lift gate on the SUV and reached in to pet Guthrie's head. His partner sat waiting to be leashed up, almost shivering as he held himself in check, waiting for the command to search. Guthrie knew what the energy of a crime scene felt like, and he was eager to work. He had no idea that his job was gruesome or sad. He simply knew the excitement of doing what he was trained to do and of being rewarded at the end of an assignment.

If only Liam could be more like his partner, able to simply do the job and set aside everything else. Lately it seemed as though so many things were piling up, distracting him. It was more than Isabella. The DGTF was a personal mission for many on the task force. Bringing the traffickers to justice would also mean bringing Kenyon Graves's killer to justice.

It was so much pressure.

He hooked Guthrie's leash to his collar, checked his partner's black vest to ensure it was properly fitted, then scratched the K-9's floppy ears. "You don't get wrapped up in all of the drama, do you, buddy? You're happy to do your job, eat some good chow, and get a decent nap."

What if he was that content with what he had? What if he could set aside the striving and the negativity?

Better yet, what if he could turn his eyes to God the way

Guthrie always watched him? What if he trusted God for guidance and provision? What if he trusted God so much that there were no worries about what might come next?

Wow. That was a convicting thought, and one he really didn't have time for when there was work to be done. It would come back to him though, in the dead of night when he couldn't sleep.

As he commanded Guthrie to exit the vehicle, Liam looked over his shoulder to where Isabella was getting out of Jenna's SUV. Yep, that thought would come back to him more than once, particularly since Isabella was temporarily back in his life.

God, I'm going to need Your help with this. My heart wants to hear her out. My head wants to walk away and forget her. Not sure what You're doing here, but a clue would be nice. This confusion was more than he could handle. He had mental and emotional whiplash, and it would have been exhausting even without all of the physical stress they'd endured.

He led Guthrie to the yellow-and-black barrier tape that ringed the area where his partner had alerted the day before. Crime scene techs waited nearby with members of the medical examiner's office, geared up with equipment at the ready to excavate the site. They'd have gone into action sooner, but given the area was an active crime scene due to Isabella's near kidnapping, they'd had to wait for clearance.

Jenna approached with a leashed Augie, while Isabella trailed behind with her arms crossed over her stomach as though she was trying to make herself smaller.

She might be the source of Liam's internal chaos, but he had to admire her strength. She was here to see this through to the end, although she had no obligation to do so and would have been safer at headquarters.

National Park Service Special Agent Emily Carroll approached with her hand extended. She was average height and build, a few years older than Liam. The investigation was under her authority. "Good to see you, Special Agent Barringer. Appreciate the helping hand. I'm on point today while Agent Givens and his team look into some other leads. He told us you were coming out for the FBI."

"Thanks." He decided to shift his thinking, to be more like Guthrie and to focus on the case instead of the woman who was now standing several feet behind him, her presence so heavy he could feel it even though she wasn't touching him. It was going to be harder than he'd expected, but he was trained and he could handle it.

He introduced Jenna and Isabella to Special Agent Carroll, though he didn't indicate who Isabella was. There was no need to bring her extra attention when she was already on edge. "And this is my partner, Guthrie. He initially alerted yesterday afternoon."

Special Agent Carroll offered Guthrie a nod. "We'd like to have him scent the area where he alerted yesterday once more before we start digging." She held up a hand. "Not questioning his abilities at all, just wanting some confirmation before we set the team to work in this heat."

"No offense taken." Guthrie was good at what he did, but there was no reason not to meet the request. It was a simple one to fulfill. "I'll also have him check the surrounding area. It seems our unsub likes it out here, and it's possible he's been operating longer than we realized. He's been escalating, so he could have started with women he hoped would go unnoticed before he decided to challenge himself by going higher profile."

"That's one of the things I'm afraid of." Special Agent Carroll surveyed the area, her eyes squinting behind her sunglasses as the morning sun rapidly heated the air. "I spent last night pulling missing person cases from the past decade for a hundred-mile radius. We have several unsolved cases, most of them the usual people who unfortunately and tragically fall off of the radar. A handful match his type with the slim build and the blond hair, but I can't say whether or not the disappearances are related."

"His type is set, but his pattern seems to be a bit random." The voice behind him was soft but authoritative. Isabella stepped up beside him and extended her hand to Carroll. "I'm a forensic sketch artist, and I've talked to the unsub's surviving kidnap victims."

"Liam said your last name is Whitmore?" Carroll shook Isabella's hand and studied her. "You were attacked last night. You offered up the detail about the boots."

He hadn't told Isabella yet, but he'd gotten several leads on the Adventure Bound boots this morning. One store in Meadowlark sold them, and the owner was going through records to see if he had any information. Adventure Bound was also going through their files and would send a list of anyone who had purchased within a hundred-mile radius once they had a warrant in place.

Isabella nodded, her face a mask of professionalism. "That was me."

The truth shuddered through him. She was in danger, was firmly in the center of a killer's radar. There was no way Liam would dangle her out there like a fish on a line, even if it meant catching a killer. He shook off the thought and urged Guthrie toward the scene where he'd alerted before.

At the tape, he covered his feet with cloth bootees handed to him by a tech who then lifted the tape enough for him to pass through with Guthrie. The space was big enough for equipment as well as multiple people who'd cleared out as they neared.

The techs stood on the fringes, watching Guthrie who was watching Liam with his tail wagging, ready to work.

This was what his partner lived for. Liam unhooked Guthrie's leash and gave him the command, the German word for *seek*. *"Suchen."*

Nose to the ground, Guthrie sniffed for several seconds, his ears nearly dragging the dirt. He sniffed extra long at one spot, then followed his nose straight to the location he'd alerted on the night before. Sitting, he looked expectantly at Liam, waiting for the treat that always came at the end of a successful hunt.

"Great job, partner." Liam enthusiastically scratched Guthrie's neck, reattached his leash, then gave him a favorite treat before directing him away from the site to avoid crime scene contamination as much as possible. While his heart always fell when they located a victim, he had to be upbeat for Guthrie, who needed positive reinforcement for a job well done.

They crossed under the crime scene tape, and he gave a curt nod of affirmation to Special Agent Carroll, who directed the crime scene techs to move in.

As soon as Guthrie finished his reward, they walked back to where Isabella waited with Jenna, who was a couple of steps away on the phone. Augie sat patiently at her feet.

Isabella watched him approach, glanced behind him where the team was beginning their work, then looked back to him, her arms still wrapped around her stomach. "This might be mildly insulting, but I was kind of hoping Guthrie was wrong yesterday."

He could appreciate the sentiment. Even Special Agent Carroll had expressed it. "It's understandable." Keeping his private life out of this public case was as hard as he'd suspected it would be. Commanding Guthrie to sit, he looked around to make sure no one—especially Jenna—was in earshot, then lowered his voice. "Look, I'm sorry I reacted last night the way I did. You threw a lot out there at once. I'm working through it."

"It's understandable." She echoed his words, though she didn't seem to notice. "I guess we'll talk later. Maybe." Her voice was flat, without hope.

He got the message. There was work to do, and he needed to focus on it. He turned away then led Guthrie back to the crime scene, showed him the barrier tape, and instructed him to keep away. He unleashed his partner. *"Suchen."*

With his nose down, Guthrie obediently searched the area, ranging farther and farther from the original scene with Liam following. The park rangers and ISB agents who weren't working watched Guthrie's progress, their tension palpable. Even Jenna, who was still on the phone, followed them with her eyes.

Guthrie ranged the area for twenty minutes, occasionally looking back at Liam, who indicated he could continue working. The longer he ranged the area without alerting, the more likely it was that there was only one body.

Liam watched Guthrie's body language, but his mind wandered. How close had Isabella come to being lost forever? He'd have never known what had happened to her, although he'd have certainly learned that she was missing.

He recentered his thinking when Guthrie looked up at him. He gave another nod of assent, and his partner slowly made his way another twenty-five feet, then fifty away from the road.

If he hadn't been here, Isabella could have died. She could have—

A change in Guthrie's demeanor severed the thought. His partner circled a small area at the base of a rock formation... and sat.

Liam's heart dropped to his boots. This was worse than they'd thought. There was another victim.

Two bodies.

Isabella pulled her sunglasses from her face and rested them on her knee as Liam took the exit that would lead them into Meadowlark, North Dakota. His task force's tech specialist, Cheyenne, had tracked down a lead on both the boots and the bracelet in Meadowlark, and they were headed there to talk to a couple of the store owners.

Four hours in the SUV with nothing but deafening silence had left her with a pounding headache. She kneaded her temples. Maybe she should have taken Daniel up on his offer to take her back to Plains City. Perhaps there she could have hidden from this nightmare for a little while.

The forensic team had tentatively identified the first body as Stephanie Parry based on a tattoo on her shoulder. No one had been surprised, but they were all saddened that the young woman's life had definitely ended at the hands of a killer.

It was hard not to take it personally when the hands of that same killer had gripped her the evening before. She shuddered.

"You okay over there?" Liam had been quiet for the entire drive. It wasn't unusual. He processed things in silence, then he drifted back into what Isabella had once termed "real life" when he had dealt with his emotions. It was tough to say whether his silence had to do with the events in the case or with her revelations the night before.

"Isabella?" Liam stopped at the light at the top of the exit ramp and looked at her. "Seriously, are you okay?"

"I'm fine." Not really, but now wasn't the time to spill her guts, not when he'd shut the door on any personal relationship between them. "It's...another body?"

"I wasn't prepared for that either." Liam navigated the turn and two more stoplights. "Given the advanced decomposition though, the second set of remains has been there for awhile. Either this guy was active long ago and something triggered him to start up again, or we found unrelated remains. That's a possibility I'm holding on to right now. The Sioux and other tribes have lived there since practically the start of history. Hikers, preppers, and outlaws have all crisscrossed that land. It could be anyone. Given that there were no clothes, no identifying markers, no nothing? And given the possible age?" He exhaled loudly. "Like I said, I'm holding out hope that we don't have another victim on our hands."

He could *hold out hope* all he wanted, but that was still a human being beneath the packed soil. Someone had lost their life at some point in time.

Death was inevitable, and right now it seemed to be everywhere. "I wish I could go home and pull the covers over my head and pretend like the past twenty-four hours never happened."

"Instead, you're stuck in an SUV with Guthrie...and me."

"That's not what I meant, and you know it." She was exhausted and overwhelmed and, like in the car with Jenna this morning, something in her snapped. "I don't think you fully understand what happened three years ago."

Liam stiffened, his knuckles turning white on the steering wheel. He breathed deeply, exhaled slowly, then breathed in again as though he was mentally counting to ten.

Maybe he should be. After all, she was the one who took off on him, but he didn't know the whole story.

Maybe that was her fault, too.

Not *maybe*. It was definitely her fault. She'd never told him.

She started to apologize yet again, her anger dying out as quickly as it had flamed, but Liam spoke first. "I can't have this conversation while I'm driving." Before she could register what was happening, he'd pulled off at a small truck stop and parked on the far side of the building, out of sight from the highway. He shifted the SUV into Park but left it running, likely to keep the AC going for both them and for Guthrie, who had gotten to his feet as soon as they'd stopped.

Liam looked over his shoulder through the metal gate at his partner. "Relax, buddy."

Immediately, Guthrie dropped, content to do exactly as Liam had asked.

Well, that made her jealous. If only she could relax so easily.

She definitely wasn't relaxed now.

Liam unfastened his seat belt and angled to face her. "Talk."

Had he ever done any interrogations? Because the set of his jaw and the stony look in his eye would probably make her confess to things she hadn't done just to take that expression off of his face.

She looked away, staring at the steering wheel.

Could she tell him the truth? Even though her father and brother were in prison and there was no longer a threat from them, her failure to trust him, her betrayal, still loomed.

He dragged his hand down his face and looked past her at something out the passenger window. "It's been three years. Whatever happened, it happened. You made a choice on your own that affected us both, and that can't be undone. How can you hurt me any more than you already have?"

The words might as well have been a punch. She felt the force of them in her chest.

Despite both of their pain though, he needed to understand. "*What happened* could have gotten you killed." She spat the words she'd been holding back for years and dared to look him in the eye.

Lines furrowed his forehead, and his eyes shifted back and forth, as though he was trying to read something in the air between them. The moment he put all of the pieces together, his jaw went slack, and his gaze slid to hers. "That's what they threatened you with, isn't it? Somebody in your family threatened to…to…?" His tone shifted upward, tacking a question mark onto his incomplete thought.

"I thought I could get away from them." She couldn't look at him. Instead, she stared at the embroidered gold *FBI* on his black polo shirt. "I thought I could have a life with you and maybe they'd never find out or maybe they wouldn't care and would leave us alone."

"But they didn't." The answer was so low she almost didn't hear it.

She knit her hands together and stared at her fingers as she twined and untwined them. "When I got home from the rehearsal dinner, my dad and my brother were in my apartment." When she'd flipped on the lights, there they'd sat, her father in her favorite reading chair and her brother settled in on the sofa like he was there to watch a football game instead of taking aim to nuke her future.

The shock had nearly made her turn and run back into the night, but she'd learned over the years how to hide her feelings, to swallow them and let them sink into her stomach instead of into her soul.

It was the same place she shoved her feelings now. "I hadn't seen or heard from them in about seven years, not since I left Savannah. I guess I thought they'd let me go, leave me alone, not bother to look for me, but as it turned out…"

"As it turned out, Christian O'Leary had kept tabs on his daughter all along."

He thought he knew, but he had no clue. "Do you remember Danielle Jakes?"

"She was one of your bridesmaids. You had classes together. She was in your sorority, right?"

"And she made a couple of hundred bucks every time she let my dad know interesting little tidbits about my life."

"Wait. What?" He dropped his hands to his lap. "She was informing on you? To a crime family?"

That had been a whole other blow on that awful night, learning that one of her closest friends wasn't actually a friend at all. How much of her life had been a lie? "He kept tabs on me every step of the way. He never intended to let me walk away, just to give me time to educate myself on my own dime. Then he figured he'd either lure me back or I'd get so tired of trying to make it on my own that I'd crawl back. When Danielle let him know that I was getting married to a soon-to-be FBI agent—"

"He saw an opportunity he couldn't resist." For the first time, Liam's expression wasn't tinged by a hint of anger.

This was the hard part, the full truth she'd never imagined she'd speak to anyone, especially not to Liam, but he was right. He deserved to know why she'd burned down their future. Tears choked her, but she pushed past them. "If I had married you, then they'd have given me six months to have you eating out of my hand and working on their side."

"And if we didn't cooperate with them?" The pain in the question was almost more than she could handle.

"Then you wouldn't have made it very long past six months." She choked on the words, desperate for him to understand. She reached across the seat and grabbed his knee. "I couldn't do that. I wouldn't do that. I chose to save your life."

He grabbed her hand and wrapped his fingers around it, holding on tightly. "I'd have done something about it. I could have—"

"Gotten yourself killed faster." She tried to pull her hand away, but he didn't let go. "I had no physical proof of what my father did, but I knew that people died mysteriously around him. Car crashes. Heart attacks. Drownings. I couldn't lose you like that. I couldn't marry you and then have to watch our backs until you were gone or, maybe worse, have them do something to destroy your name and your chances of ever making it as an FBI agent. Even if they hadn't killed you, having ties to Christian O'Leary could have prevented you from having the career you'd always dreamed of."

So she'd walked away, nuked their dreams, and destroyed his trust. All of it was something he would likely never be able to forget.

TWELVE

Liam shut off the SUV in a parking space outside of a boutique jewelry store in Meadowlark and stared at the side of the dark gray painted cinder blocks. He had zero memory of driving from the truck stop through downtown to this building. His mind had been too busy spinning with the truth he'd wondered about for years.

In short, everything he knew was wrong.

All these years, he'd wrestled and railed and anguished. All these years he'd thought Isabella had been cruel enough to simply walk away.

The truth was she'd been placed in an impossible position. She hadn't crushed him because she was cold and cruel and unfeeling.

She'd saved him because she loved him.

And she'd been the one who was crushed between a proverbial rock and a hard place.

Her story had changed everything...and yet it had changed nothing.

She still hadn't trusted him. Could he forgive her?

If he prayed this out and discovered that his feelings were still...

He couldn't even bring himself to think the word. There

were too many unknowns, and it was clear her life was in danger now from a totally different threat.

"Are we going inside?" It was the first time Isabella had spoken since she'd finished her story. Like him, she'd been silent all the way to the jewelry store.

The jewelry store that might hold the key to a killer's identity.

Okay. He had to shake off his personal issues and focus on the job. Isabella was in more immediate danger that had nothing to do with her family, and they needed to close this case quickly, before more lives were stolen by an increasingly violent killer.

"We are." He reached for the door but looked over his shoulder at her. "Are you ready?"

Shoving her blond ponytail over her shoulder, she smiled weakly. "Pretty sure he's not inside that building, so I'm good. I need to be doing something, otherwise I'm going to lose my mind thinking about how helpless I am in every part of my life."

It was obvious she was putting on a brave face even as she shared the reality of her vulnerable position. It would be awesome if he could come up with a way to comfort her, but no words came to mind.

Focus on the case. Worry about the rest later.

He opened the door, leaned back in, and commanded Guthrie to stay. Guthrie would be fine in his air-conditioned kennel with food and water at the ready.

Isabella met him at the front of the SUV. She'd dressed simply but professionally in beige linen pants and a simple white tee that somehow seemed dressier than it was. Maybe it was the silver cross that hung at her neck…

He stepped closer and looked from the charm to her eyes. He recognized that cross. He'd bought it for her on the day she was baptized six years earlier. "Have you been wearing that the whole time?" How had he not noticed it before?

Her cheeks pinked and she looked away. "I've never..." She cleared her throat. "I've never taken it off."

The words punched him squarely in the chest. She'd continued to wear his ring and the cross he'd given her. She hadn't forgotten him or tossed him away. She'd carried him close the entire time they'd been apart.

What was he supposed to do with this information?

Nothing right now. There were more pressing matters to attend to.

Turning away from her, he pulled the shop's glass door open and ushered her into the air-conditioned space.

The shop was small but comfortable. The glass door was flanked by two tall, narrow windows that let in light, though they were protected by heavy decorative metal grating meant to prevent break-ins. A comfy chair and plant sat in front of each window. A long counter spanned the narrow room with enough space on one end to squeeze past to the rear of the shop. Behind the counter, a large space opened up into a workshop with a large fabric-covered table in the center, covered in tools of the trade. A counter ran around the edge of the workspace with cabinets above and below. A door behind it likely led to storage or office space.

Everything was cluttered, but neat.

At the sound of the bell over the door, a man walked in from the back.

He was nothing like Liam had expected, although he tried not to carry preconceived notions about anyone. That only hampered investigations.

This man was young, probably not much older than Liam's twenty-eight years. A thick Viking-red beard covered the lower half of his face, and he was built like a football linebacker. If the man produced an axe and started talking about logging, no one would bat an eye.

As the man approached, his welcoming smile softened his gruff exterior. "Hi, my name is Rhys Baker. How can I help you two?"

Liam shook off his surprise and held his credentials up for Rhys to inspect. "I'm Special Agent Liam Barringer, and this is forensic artist Isabella Whitmore."

She stood slightly behind him, watching them talk.

The man's brown eyes lit with recognition. "Yes, I spoke to you earlier about the bracelet."

Rhys walked to the worktable and came back with a slim laptop. He seemed to pick up on Liam's surprise that he was the jeweler. "I caught the jewelry bug young, when I was on a trip with my grandfather to Arizona and watched the Navajo make jewelry. I apprenticed with several different jewelers around the country and now, here I am, blowing people's minds." He chuckled, then sobered. "I'm pretty sure you're looking for information and not my history, though. What can I help the FBI with? You said you're looking for a specific bracelet? One that you saw online?"

"Yes. Isabella drew an image of the bracelet in question, and we ran a reverse image search. An image popped up on your gallery page that closely matches her drawing. We were hoping you'd remember who you sold it to."

"I'll take a look. I remember pretty much everything I make, especially if it was custom." Rhys opened the laptop. "Can I see the photo?"

Liam opened his phone and thumbed to the digital copy of the image Isabella had drawn, then slid it across the counter for Rhys to see.

Leaning over, Rhys studied the drawing but didn't touch

the phone. When he lifted his head, it was to look behind Liam at Isabella. "You drew this?"

"I did." Her voice was quiet but confident. She'd always been aware of her talent, though she'd never been prideful.

Rhys studied Isabella in a way that made Liam check his hands for scars. He was showing way too much interest in her. There were a few that looked like old cuts or small burns, but nothing like Isabella and the other women had described.

Finally, Rhys smiled. "You're very good. I could use a designer if you ever want to freelance anything. I'm always looking for new ideas."

"Thanks." Isabella's voice also held a smile. "But I'm pretty happy where I am."

Interesting. She was happy as a forensic sketch artist. He wondered what had made her choose that career instead of pursuing her original plan of doing murals and paintings for historic sites and museums? Was she trying to atone for her family? Something he'd have to ask later, when things quieted down...

If they were still speaking when this was all over.

"Helping others. That's admirable." Rhys nodded and looked down at Liam's phone. "Yeah, so, the bracelet. I do remember that one." He typed something into the keyboard and dragged a finger over the track pad. "Sold it about two years ago to a local woman who wanted it for her boyfriend. It's a rope because they used to rock climb together. The stones are polished and came from some of the places where they used to climb. And the crystal flame is, well..." Rhys dragged his hand across his chin then turned the laptop so they could see it.

The bracelet in the photo was a thick silver braided rope that was linked together every inch or so by polished stones of varying colors.

Isabella leaned over Liam's shoulder to look. She gasped then stepped back. "That's it." The fear in her voice iced the air in the room.

Rhys looked up.

Liam wanted to kick himself. He should have prepared her for this. He should have shown her the image Cheyenne had found instead of simply telling her about it. Then she might have been prepared to see in clear, photographic evidence the bracelet belonging to the man who had nearly ended her life.

He wanted to reach for her, but he couldn't. Not in front of Rhys Baker. This had to stay professional.

Forcing his posture to remain straight, he focused on Rhys. "What were you saying about the flame?"

Rhys looked away from Isabella and turned the laptop back to face himself, then punched a few more keys. "She said her boyfriend had been through a 'trial by fire,' and it ended their rock-climbing days. She wanted the bracelet so he'd always remember that, no matter what happened, she'd be his rock."

That was either really sweet or really sappy. Or, given that the boyfriend in question was likely a serial killer, it might be really twisted. "Can you give me her name? Maybe a phone number?" This was the tricky part. Rhys could demand a court order, or he could simply be helpful and hand it over.

"Yeah." Rhys closed the laptop, and Liam's heart sank. Closing the machine meant he wasn't going to hand over the information.

Liam steeled himself for a legal discussion.

"No need to give you a number." Rhys jerked a thumb toward the back door. "Her name's Jeralyn Locke. I don't know her well, and I never met the boyfriend because he didn't live in Meadowlark, but she's a paralegal over at the law office on Twelfth. She did some work for my dad when he was setting up his LLC."

Twelfth Street was only a couple of blocks away...

Which meant answers might be around the corner.

Could they really be this close to putting an end to this waking nightmare?

Isabella kept close to Liam as they walked up the street. The midafternoon heat hung heavy and stifling between the buildings along the historic downtown street. Narrow sidewalks were crowded with tourists who had come to the area for history, shopping, and outdoor activities around Meadowlark.

She couldn't help but eye all of the men, sizing them up to see if they matched the build of the man who had tried to take her, staring at their arms and hands in search of burn scars. If they were this close, he could be anywhere, watching her.

The idea ran chills across her skin. A thousand eyes stared at her, searing the back of her head with their intensity.

Instinctively, she reached for Liam's hand. She needed something solid to hold on to, something to protect her, something to keep her from stumbling headfirst into a raging panic attack.

His fingers laced through hers, and he drew her to his side. They stepped around a knot of teenagers who stared into the window of a comic-book store, debating loudly whether to go there or the bakery next door.

When they'd passed the group, Liam leaned toward her to whisper in her ear. "Are you doing okay?"

Her fingers tightened around his, and she shook her head. No, she was not. Not in the least. It had only been ten minutes since the jeweler had given them confirmation that he'd made the bracelet her would-be kidnapper—killer—wore. She hadn't had time to process, and now she was on a crowded street as a moving target.

Again.

Liam stopped on the sidewalk, and several people stepped around them as he looked up and down the street, searching. Tugging her hand, he led her past several doors then suddenly diverted into an alcove surrounded by windows filled with displays of books. He opened the door between the windows and ushered her into a wonderful, chilled space that smelled slightly of mildew and heavily of ink and paper.

She pulled in a deep breath and closed her eyes as he led her deeper into the store, trusting him not to let her fall.

Her eyes flew open as he guided her farther from the windows.

She still trusted him not to let her fall.

As they rounded a corner between two tall bookcases, her gasp stopped him. Turning, he gripped her shoulders and scanned her face. "Did something happen?" His frantic gaze roamed her face, searching for injury.

"I'm fine." Taking a deep breath, she stepped away from his touch. "I just need a minute." Or an hour. Or a day. Or maybe a year.

"You're right. I'm sorry." Liam reached behind his back and tested the sturdiness of the floor-to-ceiling bookshelf before he leaned back against it. "I forget you're law-enforcement-*adjacent* and not used to sprinting ahead while chasing down leads. It's a lot to process that your attacker might be close by." He pulled his phone out. "I need to let Special Agent Carroll know what's going on, and then I'll have someone on the team come back and get you. There's no need for you to—"

"It's fine. I want to go." She wanted—no, needed—to see the woman who loved a killer enough to have a bracelet made for him and to promise to stand by him. She likely had no way of knowing that the man she loved was assaulting and killing women. "I need to process for a second. It felt like...like there were eyes around every corner." Not to mention her heart was beating triple time because of Liam.

"You felt like you were being watched?" Pocketing his phone without using it, he straightened and walked to the end of the row to look toward the door. "No one followed us in."

"It was paranoia." She studied his back as he scanned the store, protecting her.

He had always protected her. He'd been the one she ran to when she was scared, even when he didn't fully understand why. There had been one night when she'd been convinced she spotted her brother at a burger place in town.

Liam hadn't understood her fear when she'd pounded on the door to his dorm room, tearful and shaken. He didn't even know she had a brother, and she couldn't tell him why seeing her family would terrify her, but he'd held her close and told her he loved her no matter what.

That had been the first time he'd told her that. It had been the moment she'd realized that she had more than God in her life to walk beside her—she also had Liam. It was the first time she'd said *I love you* to him as well.

He'd protected her then. Maybe she should have trusted him to protect her when her father and brother came calling. Maybe she really had been wrong to run away, to try to carry the load herself when they might have been meant to carry it together.

And now?

She still trusted him to protect her. Still felt whole when he was near.

Turning her face toward the ceiling, Isabella bit her lower lip. She still loved him. She'd never stopped. Leaving him had nearly killed her. She'd managed to bury her feelings under work, but her heart had never stopped beating for him.

She dropped her gaze to him. Not that he would ever trust her again.

As though he could feel her watching, he looked over his shoulder. He walked back the couple of feet with a concerned expression on his face. "Tell me what's going on, Izzy."

Izzy. She hated that nickname from anyone but him. Somehow, from him, it always sounded right.

Breathe in. Breathe out. "Liam, I'm sorry."

Compassion softened his features. "Don't apologize. Taking a second to process this is natural. Being scared is natural. You've been through a lot of trauma in the past—"

"No." This was the absolute wrong time to be confessing, but all of her defensive layers had been peeled away in the past twenty-four hours. She had nothing left to hide behind. "You were right. I should have talked to you. I should have run to you instead of running away. It wasn't my place to make that decision for both of us."

She'd never seen anyone actually look *stunned* before, but Liam came close. His eyes widened, and although his mouth remained closed, his jaw seemed to slacken. He froze, watching her as though he'd never seen something so rare or beautiful or shocking in his life.

He balled his fists and held them away from his sides before dropping them against his thighs. His expression shifted from surprise to what might be torture. The lines in his forehead and around his mouth deepened. "I can't do this."

He was right, and she shouldn't ask him to forgive her. She'd wounded him deeply and now they were in a battle for her life and—

"Izzy." His voice dropped to a whisper, and he stepped closer, closing the gap between them. His hands ran up her arms, across her shoulders, into her hair… His head tipped forward until his lips nearly met hers. "I can't do this." The words were a breath on her lips…

And she met him the rest of the way.

THIRTEEN

He drew Isabella closer, and the rest of the world vanished.

The last three years vanished.

There was nothing but right here, right now.

Nothing about her had changed since the last time he'd kissed her, when he'd told her *See you tomorrow* on the night before their wedding.

The night before she'd broken his heart.

Did that even matter anymore? Given what he'd told her?

All he wanted was this moment. This now. This forever. Her. Him.

He wanted everything to be like it used to be.

He wanted—

Someone cleared their throat to his right.

Isabella jerked back, whacking her head against the bookshelf as Liam turned toward the sound, stepping away from her and preparing to go to battle. What had he been thinking, letting his guard down? Kissing her? And now—

A very embarrassed teenager stood at the end of the aisle, her cheeks red and her eyes wide. She aimed a finger at the bookcase behind him. "I'm, um, can I…" She took a deep breath and gave a sheepish smile. "Could I get to the books that are right there? And then I'll…go." Her finger shifted to point behind her.

Isabella backed up the aisle slowly, moving away from the girl. She grabbed his hand and drew him with her. "It's fine." Her face was the color of a ripe strawberry. "We're leaving. You can have the whole shelf." She tugged him to the end of the bookcase, down two more aisles, and to a small café in the back of the store where she dropped his hand and took a seat in a chair facing the rear of the building. She buried her face in her hands. "That was…"

Incredible? Something I had never thought would happen again? Something exactly right?

She exhaled loudly and spoke into her palms. "That was so, so wrong."

"Wrong?" He slid into the chair across from her, wanting to reach for her but not daring to. His hopes crashed. If she thought kissing him was wrong, how was this going to play out?

"Liam." Her voice was muffled behind her hands. "We kissed in the young adult section of a bookstore."

Wait. Was *that* the part she thought was wrong? Not the kiss itself?

Yes, this was an odd and even dangerous situation in more ways than one. Yes, they had a lot to talk about, but he wasn't sure he could say he regretted anything that had just happened, not now that he knew the truth about why she'd left.

Which was still considerably more complicated than he wanted to admit. "Izzy?"

She parted her index and middle fingers to peek at him. "What?"

"You're right, but I'm not sorry." Not in the least. Maybe the timing was wrong and the place was certainly wrong, but what he was feeling? That wasn't wrong. He was drawn to her in the same way he always had been. Learning how much she'd suffered on his behalf tugged at his heart. She may have done things the wrong way, in a way he never would have chosen, but she'd made those choices to protect him. She'd never set out to harm him. Love had driven her to sacrifice herself for him.

How was he supposed to handle this?

Slowly, Isabella lowered her hands from her face and dropped them into her lap. For a long time, she stared at him as though she was trying to read his sincerity. "Now what?"

He'd love to say they could sit here and talk everything out, decide if they wanted to let the past be history and start over, or if things were too irreparably broken to even consider moving forward.

Everything in him hoped that walking away from one another was off the table.

At the same time, his emotions were spinning in a giant tornado, and he wasn't sure about starting over either.

Like the aftermath of a tornado, everything was a chaotic mess.

And everything was happening in the middle of too many open cases, which lay squarely in his hands. He had to focus on them above everything else, at least at the moment. He had to set aside personal for professional. "Right now, nothing happens. Not with us."

Her gaze dropped to the wooden table, which was scarred with scratched-in names, initials, and hearts. Clearly, the bookstore encouraged the minor vandalism, or at least they didn't *discourage* it.

"Izzy." He wanted to move his chair around to her side of the table, but he didn't. She was a danger to his rational mind. "I don't mean forever. I mean right now there are more pressing matters. We have to walk up the street and talk to…" He glanced around to make sure they hadn't picked up any eavesdroppers. No one was near but, out of an abundance of caution, he kept things vague. "To talk to someone who might have answers. Someone who might be able to put a stop to what's happening before someone else gets hurt."

She nodded, her gaze fixed on the table. "You're right." When she finally looked up, a soft smile lifted her lips. Lips he'd love to kiss again. "I'm usually more professional than this. I don't typically go around kissing the law enforcement officers I'm working with."

The unexpected comment loosened the vise around his heart. As he stood, he looked down at her as he chuckled. "Boy, I hope not." He started to reach for her hand as she stood, but professionalism demanded they not touch again.

Instead, he ushered her ahead of him out the door and to the sidewalk. He kept her protectively close as they walked up the street to the law office where Jeralyn Locke worked.

The air-conditioning was cool as they stepped into the historic storefront. A modern lobby greeted him, all glass and metal, a stark contrast to the historic weathered brick exterior of the building. Behind a gleaming counter, a young man who appeared to be in his midtwenties looked up from a computer screen. "Good afternoon. Do you have an appointment with one of our attorneys?"

Liam kept his credentials tucked away for the moment. Flashing them too soon in a law office could put everyone on edge enough to stonewall him, and this guy seemed trained to be the guard at the gate. "We were actually hoping to see Jeralyn?"

"Oh, okay." The polished facade fell away, and the man smiled. "She just got back from the courthouse. I'll run and get her." He was gone before Liam could react to the man's about-face in character.

"Okay, then." Isabella's voice was low and slightly amused. "I guess they only trained him to a point."

"Guess so." Either that or he'd been taught to protect the big bosses' time while letting everyone else confront the public. Who knew? Liam was just grateful it had been easy.

The man from the desk reappeared in the hallway and waved a friendly hand at a cluster of chairs in the corner. "She's putting away her stuff. She'll be out in a second if you want to take a seat."

No way. He felt way more prepared for whatever came his way if he was on his feet.

He turned to ask Isabella if she wanted to sit, but a soft rustle from the hallway stopped him.

Isabella stared over his shoulder, her expression suddenly slack and her eyes wide.

He turned as a woman stopped at the side of the reception counter. She was tall, with striking hazel eyes and straight blond hair that hung past her shoulders.

She looked almost exactly like Isabella.

What was happening? Isabella grabbed the back of Liam's shirt, afraid her knees might give way.

While the woman standing by the counter wasn't her twin by any means, the similarities were still striking. Their builds were similar. Jeralyn's eyes could have been her own. And their blond hair could have been styled by the same person.

Jeralyn Locke's eyes widened and she took a step back, her gaze flicking to Liam before returning to Isabella. Reaching out, she grabbed the edge of the counter as her face went pale.

The young man behind the reception counter stood. "Jeralyn? Are you okay?"

She smiled weakly. "Sorry, Clint. I walked over from the courthouse too fast and it made me lightheaded. I'll be fine."

She took a deep breath, let go of the counter, and stiffened her spine. "We can talk in the conference room, if you'd like?"

Was that the best idea? Jeralyn seemed to know exactly who she was or at least to understand that something was happening. What if this was a trap?

Be realistic, Isabella. In a law office? Surely not.

But what if the man who had attacked her was a lawyer and was in the building right now? What if—

Liam's hand on the small of her back clamped a lid on her fears. She wasn't alone. Liam was right beside her. He'd protected her so far, and she trusted he'd continue to do so.

They followed Jeralyn up the hallway, where she opened the door to a large conference room.

The space was walled in on three sides with glass. The fourth wall held bookcases that contained the obligatory volumes of law books that seemed to take up space in every law office on the planet. This was apparently the central hub of the office, as the hallway went down both sides, with office doors and glass-fronted offices facing the conference room.

Anyone looking for visual privacy wasn't going to find it here, although, when Jeralyn closed the door behind them, the silence was nearly complete.

Still pale, she walked around the table and took a seat, her hands shaking. "Please, sit." She glanced around as though she expected to see eyes at every corner.

What was Jeralyn thinking and feeling? She sat in the chair closest to the door.

Liam stood behind her, looking across the gleaming wooden table at Jeralyn. "I won't drag this out, Ms. Locke. I'm FBI Agent Liam Barringer, but you seem to suspect that already."

Her gaze dropped. She drew her fingertip along the edge

of the table. "I'm at the courthouse enough to recognize a law enforcement officer when I see one."

Liam moved to stand beside Isabella and laid his credentials on the table. He slid them into Jeralyn's line of sight and let her get a good look before he pocketed them and rested his hand on the back of Isabella's chair.

He was protecting her. The realization both warmed and chilled her. He was standing between her and the door and was directly facing Jeralyn. He didn't trust this woman, and he was going to be first in the line of fire if someone came after Isabella.

Her stomach dropped. Liam was risking his life because of her. All of her running from her family, leaving him behind, and turning her back on their life together hadn't done a thing to protect him. He was in danger at any given time, no matter what she did to mitigate it.

But he was also safe at any given time, no matter what she did. Whether she was standing between him and death or not, God was. His job was inherently dangerous, but God had protected him. God would continue to protect him.

Despite the tension in the glassed-in room, Isabella relaxed. For the first time in three years, her mind shifted into a lower gear, and her emotions didn't feel as though they were running at double speed.

For the first time in three years, she felt peace.

It was almost unsettling, given that she was sitting squarely in what could be loosely defined as an interrogation.

She pulled her thoughts back into the room, where Jeralyn was staring at her.

Liam broke the silence. He slid his phone across the table to Jeralyn, the screen open to the photo of the bracelet taken from Rhys's website. "You purchased this for someone. Would you tell us who it was?"

There was a tense stretch of silence as Jeralyn studied the photo, then she shoved the phone back to Liam. "Am I in trouble? Do I need a lawyer?" She kept her hands flat on the table, but her gaze swept the office doors along the hallway. "Everyone here is in real estate, but they have friends I can call." She looked frightened, her hazel eyes wide. There was no defiance, only questions and fear.

Liam pocketed his phone. "No one suspects you of anything. I'm here about the man you gave this bracelet to. It's one of a kind, and several victims of a crime have noted that their attacker wore a bracelet like this." He looked at the photo as though he was studying it, but Isabella knew him well enough to know he was letting his words settle. "They also mentioned severe burn scars on the man's hands and forearms. Given that you told the jeweler that the recipient had been through a *trial by fire*, we would like to have a conversation with him."

"I was afraid of this." Jeralyn stared at her hands, then her eyes closed. "I dated a man for a while. We met online. We both enjoyed rock climbing. He was burned in..." She looked up, her face pale. "He told me it was an accident in his shed, but I started to wonder." Her gaze drifted to the hallway, where a man exited an office, glanced in their direction, and continued on.

Isabella wanted to walk around the table and shake the story out of Jeralyn. *Who is he? Where is he?*

Jeralyn looked up at Liam, her posture suddenly rigid. "He kept watching other women. Kept talking to them and pursuing them, even though he said he loved me. I broke up with him. He tried to convince me not to leave. Kept following me... And I came here. He won't look for me here."

"That makes no sense. You have a prior association with

Meadowlark. You bought the bracelet here." Liam leaned forward. "Who is he? And why wouldn't he look for you here?"

"He never knew where I bought it. I found the jeweler online. The only time I ever came here before I moved here was to pick up the bracelet." She picked at a cuticle, then balled her fists. "I had to get away from him after I found…" She stood so fast that the chair teetered and threatened to fall before it righted itself. "This feels off. I'm not saying more without a lawyer."

Liam inched closer to Isabella. "That's your right, but this man seems to be targeting women who look like you, and he's been taking them from Meadowlark. I'm sure you've heard. I'm sure you suspect. We need his name in order to make him stop."

"No." Jeralyn shook her head again. "Lawyer."

Isabella stood and bit down on her tongue to keep from begging for the man's name. Clearly something he'd done had traumatized Jeralyn. Why wouldn't she say his name? Why wouldn't she help stop him?

Liam pulled a card from his pocket and laid it on the table. "If you change your mind, call me." He walked toward the door, motioning for Isabella to follow.

No. They were so close. She practically stumbled as she walked to the door, her eyes wide with questions, but he avoided her gaze.

As he opened the door, he turned back to Jeralyn. "I'm here to help, Jeralyn. If you want us to put a stop to what he's doing, just call. I promise we can protect you." He turned toward the hall, his gaze sweeping past Isabella.

This made no sense. She stepped into the hallway. The answer was right in front of them. Was it because Jeralyn had asked for a lawyer? What was happening?

Liam followed her into the hallway and the door started to close.

"Wait." Jeralyn's choked voice stopped them.

The door hit Liam in the shoulder as he turned, and Isabella whirled around.

Jeralyn stood halfway between the table and the door, wringing her hands. She dug her teeth into her lip and shook her head with tears in her eyes. "His name is Steven. Steven Newman."

FOURTEEN

"Steven Newman lives near Prospector Rock." Liam pointed to a map projected on the wall in the conference room of the Ziebach County, South Dakota courthouse, where they were setting up to raid Newman's property. The little community of Prospector Rock was little more than an unincorporated dot on the county's map, but it was poised to become one of the most notorious locations in the state if the evidence was true and Steven Newman proved to be their man.

He looked back toward the table in the small room, where a team of deputies from several counties, fellow FBI agents, and Park Service ISB agents watched him carefully, ready to move on his command.

Somewhere up the hallway in a break room, Isabella was with Jenna, waiting for his order to transfer to Daniel's house, where she should be safe until this was all over.

How had he ended up in charge of this raid?

He knew how. On the DGTF, he had already built relationships across agencies, and the lead agents valued those relationships. Given that the serial killer case shared a thread with their trafficking case, select members of the DGTF were also working alongside the team on this raid.

They were moving out in short order to converge on property owned by Steven Newman. They'd sent two deputies to scout ahead, and Newman was on the property, or he had been an hour ago.

The guy had been on no one's radar. He'd never had so much as a parking ticket.

Cheyenne had more resources at her disposal and a smaller case load than her counterparts with other agencies, so she'd run checks on Newman as soon as Liam had walked out of the law office and called her.

At thirty-four, Newman was a model citizen on paper. According to public records, he'd been a lineman for a local power company near Plains City until a fire on his property left him with horrific burns over most of his hands, arms, and torso. He'd moved to Prospector Rock shortly after, taking random jobs on local ranches, although he'd kept largely to himself.

The real story could be found between the lines. According to Jeralyn, they'd started dating about six years earlier. She'd broken up with him three years ago, before the fire on his property, and they'd reunited shortly after. They'd parted ways again a few months earlier. The victims were all blond-haired, hazel-eyed women who favored Jeralyn. She'd refused to say more without a lawyer.

Isabella and the two kidnapping victims had been shown photos of Steven Newman, and all agreed he matched the build of the man who had attacked them and that the scars seemed to match up. Isabella had also noted that the eyes were the same brown as her attempted kidnapper's. Based on Jeralyn's statement, receipts that proved Newman had ordered Adventure Bound boots directly from the company, and the witnesses' confirmations, a judge had issued the warrant for Newman's arrest.

It was clear that Steven was obsessed with Jeralyn, and

he likely took out his frustrations over their breakups on women who favored her.

Hopefully, his days of tormenting her doppelgängers were about to end. With warrants in place, the team was ready to roll.

While Daniel had cleared Cheyenne and the tech team to assist on the kidnapping case, he'd have also loved to have the rest of his DGTF team members backing him. Jurisdiction was a tricky thing though, and they wanted to be sure everything was buttoned down and unquestionable. As it was, they'd all reached out to offer prayers, advice, and words of encouragement from the moment Cheyenne had notified them that he was leading a multijurisdictional raid.

As soon as everything was clear and Steven Newman was in custody, Guthrie would search the property for bodies Newman might have buried closer to home.

Lord, don't let there be more bodies.

The team broke apart, preparing to move out to the assembly location near Newman's property, which was located on a large wooded lot at the back of an older neighborhood.

When the room was empty, Liam sat down at the head of the table and prayed.

No one could predict what would happen in a raid like this. Steven Newman was the suspect in multiple kidnappings and murders. He likely wouldn't go quietly.

On the table, his phone buzzed. He glanced at the screen to see who was calling.

Officer Jack Donadio was helping Cheyenne with tech duties while he recovered from a gunshot wound to the leg, so if he was calling instead of texting, he had important intel.

Liam broke off his prayers and picked up the phone. "You have something for me, Jack?"

"Yes and no." Jack was a friendly guy and one of their

team leader's—Daniel's—closest friends. He was popular with the rest of the team, and they were all cheering him on as he recovered. "First of all, the second body Guthrie alerted on appears to be unrelated. It's likely someone who was buried out there decades or even more than a century ago, based on evidence found with the remains."

That was a relief. At least they could spare another family some heartache.

But Jack had said he had more. "What else?"

"Cheyenne and I have been going through Newman's bank and cell phone records. I'll spare you the details since you're about to head out, but he's got phone calls and credit card transactions that line up with the times that the women went missing in Meadowlark. It's looking more and more like he's your guy."

"I hope so. This needs to end before someone else becomes a victim." If Steven Newman wasn't successful in getting to Isabella soon, he might move on to someone else, someone who didn't have a protector with the power of the FBI and the DGTF in her corner.

"Also, when Cheyenne and I ran his financials, we got a hit to a physical therapist in Plains City. Care to guess who else we've been tracking who also had some transactions hit at that office?"

Liam sat up taller, his heart rate rising. This was about to get interesting. "Who?"

"Brody Patterson."

"Calista Franklin's boyfriend. The first murder victim we found." Brody had ties to the trafficking ring as a low-level runner. "Is there any evidence that Steven Newman is involved in gunrunning?" Were they about to blow two cases open on the same day? Were they closer than ever to ending this ring? To finding out who had killed Kenyon Graves?

"No," Jack said. "We don't have anything to link him to anyone else in the ring, but we cross-referenced their card info and found two different occasions when they ate at the same sports bar on the same day at the same time."

"So Newman could have spotted Calista with Brody at the PT office then targeted her from that moment. It's possible he befriended Brody in an effort to get closer to her."

"At the very least, he followed them to lunch and was watching them." Jack exhaled loudly. "At any rate, let your team know to keep their eyes open when you go in. It's not likely that Newman has anything to do with our traffickers, but we can't be totally certain either."

"How big is this weapons ring? It seems like everything we touch lately has some bizarre connection to it."

"It's getting kind of scary, no doubt." Jack was tapping away at a keyboard, already distracted, but the sound stopped suddenly. "Listen, man, I'm praying for you guys. Get in, get this dude, and get out safe."

"Will do." Liam killed the call and stared at the dark screen. Jack had every right to express concern. His recovery had been anything but easy. He'd suffered several setbacks and was facing yet another surgery if things didn't improve. Jack was a good cop who should be in the field with his K-9 partner, Beau, although he'd become a rock star at helping Cheyenne on the tech side of the house.

"Got a minute?"

His gaze went to the door at the sound of Isabella's voice. She stood just inside the room, her hands knit together in front of her.

Tense lines in her forehead and around her mouth spoke volumes about the toll Newman's attacks were taking on her. The lack of sleep, overwhelming threats, and drama were heavy in her eyes, which also bore lines around them.

At some point, she'd taken out her contacts and put on her glasses. With her hair up in a ponytail, she looked a lot like she had in college when she'd pulled all-nighters to finish art projects or to study for exams.

Just like in the bookstore earlier, time seemed to zip backward. In this space, in this moment, they were still twenty and their entire future stretched out before them. She was still his, and he was still hers. He was madly, irrevocably in love with her.

That wasn't a historical fact. It was a present reality. The truth he'd been reluctant to admit settled in and quieted his heart. It was high time he stopped fighting what he couldn't change.

He'd never stopped loving her.

But could he trust her? She'd hidden so much from him... had refused to share her very big problems with him...had shut him out of major life decisions. Would she—

"Liam?" She stepped farther into the room, one delicate eyebrow arching above the frame of her dark glasses. "Is everything okay?"

Clearly he'd been staring at her for too long. "It's fine. I have a lot on my mind." He needed to focus on the upcoming raid, not on his conflicted feelings for Isabella.

Once again, she was distracting him from the immediate threat.

She nodded, her ponytail swinging. "I'm sure you do. I just wanted to see you before you left. One of the deputies came in and told Jenna you're about to head out."

"We are." He stood and crossed his arms, keeping the table between them. It was dangerous for himself and his team if he tangled up his personal and professional lives. "Jenna is going to take you back to Daniel's place near Plains City, and I'll see you there after this is all done. You'll be safe there. He's built in a lot of security measures. That's the kind of guy Daniel is." He ached to walk across the room and pull her close, but he was also afraid to fully let her in.

If he touched her, he might never want to leave, not with his emotions bouncing all over the place. If he thought they had a future, he might hesitate in the clutch today. It was time to put on his game face.

She started to speak, and then stopped. Tilting her head, she gave him a soft, sad smile. "Come back safe."

"I will."

With a look so long she seemed to be memorizing his face, she disappeared up the hall, taking a piece of his heart with her.

Liam stood in the center of Steven Newman's living room, turning a slow circle as the rest of the team made their way slowly back through the house. He stopped when he faced the front door, where a pair of Adventure Bound boots rested next to a stack of unopened shipping boxes.

Despite intel to the contrary, Newman wasn't home. Given that a bowl of macaroni and cheese was still warm on the kitchen table, he'd fled quickly moments before they'd arrived on scene. Either he'd installed cameras that they'd missed, or he'd heard them coming.

Or, worse, maybe Jeralyn Locke wasn't as distant from her ex as she'd claimed.

He'd already put in a call to the police department in Meadowlark to have Jeralyn brought in for further questioning. It wasn't that he didn't believe her story—it was that he didn't believe anyone, not wholeheartedly.

Isabella had trained him well in that regard.

Shaking off thoughts of her, he walked to the window and watched the late afternoon shadows dance among the trees in the woods that surrounded the property. Something moved from left to right, abasing the wind.

He leaned closer to the window. Was that a person?

The shadow disappeared quickly, a trick of the shifting light. Still, he should go—

"Agent Barringer, you should see this." The call came from the door at the rear of the house.

He strode through the kitchen and to the back door, where a deputy waited at the bottom of cracked concrete steps that led down to a small overgrown backyard. The local officer was holding a heavy metal flashlight.

Weeds and small trees had long ago choked out the grass, and patches of dirt spread among the overgrowth. Several metal sheds dotted the property, running all the way back into the trees. The doors to each stood open, each having already been searched by the team.

The deputy looked up at him, his face a mask of stone. "I think we found your proof, or at least enough to put this guy away for a long time." He started walking toward one of the sheds, a dark gray metal building about six feet by eight feet that stood at the back center of the yard. "As soon as we finish sweeping the area and get the high sign from you, we'll get the crime scene techs in here."

This was not good if they were talking about CSI. "More bodies?"

"No, but..." The deputy stopped at the shed door and aimed his flashlight at the interior of the dark space.

Liam stepped up, steeling himself for what he'd find inside.

The interior of the small shed was dark and stifling. The windows had been boarded over from the outside. The walls, floor, and ceiling were covered in plywood painted black. The flashlight beam illuminated a camping cot covered in dirty navy blue blankets. A bucket beside the bed was the only other item in the room.

But the most chilling discovery was the two sets of handcuffs attached to chains that ran through small holes to the outside of the building.

Swallowing bile, he looked away.

The deputy had followed his gaze. "They're anchored to metal poles outside of the shed. Obviously, we haven't been inside for a closer inspection, but I'm guessing there's soundproofing between that plywood and the exterior walls."

Liam stepped away from the hopelessness of the shed and stared at the sky, breathing deep lungfuls of the fresh air that Steven Newman's captives had been denied. "He kept them in there." He'd read the victims' statements about the complete sensory deprivation of their prison, about how their captor only came at night and how complete the darkness always was. They'd never been able to see him. Both of them had spoken of the panic and mind-twisting uncertainty that came from no sound, no light, and oppressive heat.

Seeing the space in real time made his stomach threaten to revolt. What horrors had those women endured?

He didn't dare let his mind grasp that Isabella could have been chained inside of that nightmare.

That was the last thing he needed to imagine.

He turned to the deputy. "What about the rest of the sheds?"

"Nothing like this." The deputy looked as grim and sick as Liam felt. He turned his back on the doorway and, like Liam, seemed to relish the fresh air.

That was a blessing. "Wait here until the crime scene techs arrive, and make certain no one enters the building. Call the sheriff and give her an update, then have her reach out to the heads of the other agencies. I'm going to get my partner and check the area." There was no need to say what he was searching for. Everyone was aware of Guthrie's specialty.

They all hoped the K-9's never-miss nose wouldn't find a reason to alert.

His heart was heavy as he opened the back of the SUV and walked toward the rear of the property with Guthrie at his side, watching his every move.

Liam battled a soul-deep disappointment. He'd really hoped to end this today. With Newman on the run and his home swarmed by a task force dedicated to taking him down, there was no telling when the man would surface again. He might continue to target Isabella, or he might go to ground for years before the urge to kill overtook him and he terrorized more women and stole more lives.

They had to find Newman before he killed again.

Liam led Guthrie to the woods behind the shed, which was the likely place Newman might have buried earlier victims. He made eye contact with Guthrie, who watched expectantly, knowing the hunt was on. *"Suchen."*

Immediately, Guthrie dropped his nose to the ground and sniffed, moving in wide circles.

The bulk of the team had moved to the front of the house to wait for the crime scene investigators, not wanting to disturb potential evidence. The only person present was the deputy who guarded the shed where Newman had kept his prisoners. The man watched Guthrie with interest for a few minutes before taking a return phone call from the sheriff and providing the update Liam had instructed him to give.

Liam listened to the deputy for a moment, then followed Guthrie, who doubled back toward the sheds, sniffing around the outsides but not showing any interest. That was a good indication that wherever Calista Franklin and Stephanie Parry had been killed, it wasn't in one of the sheds. Guthrie would have picked up on a residual scent, had that been the case. His nose was sensitive enough to sniff out any place remains had been, even if they'd been moved months before.

Interesting that the women hadn't died where they'd been held. Nor had they seemingly been killed where their remains were found. Somewhere out there was a whole other crime scene.

Guthrie ranged deeper into the trees, occasionally looking up at Liam to see if the command had changed, then moving forward at a motion from Liam's hand. Guthrie sniffed his way back toward the house, coming up on the western side before following his nose back into the woods, ranging deeper this time.

Either he was on to something or he'd determined that the yard held no interest and was searching for more. Guthrie was trained to scent only on human remains and, while he might pause to investigate an animal, he wouldn't alert.

They were fairly deep into the trees and had been searching for nearly half an hour. Clearly they were getting nowhere. He needed to take Guthrie back to scent in a different—

Guthrie stopped and raised his head, but he looked past Liam, not at him. His nose twitched.

Liam turned to see what had gotten his partner's attention.

A twig snapped.

A shadow moved to his right.

A force drove him to the ground.

He landed hard on his back and tried to swing, but someone jumped on top of him and wrapped heavy hands around his neck before he could cry out or fight back.

Barking wildly, Guthrie pawed at the man who pinned Liam. He was not trained to attack and would only go so far to defend.

The man ignored Guthrie, staring down at Liam with angry, determined dark eyes. His facial features registered through the roar in Liam's head. Steven Newman.

And he had the upper hand.

Liam struggled and fought, clawing at Newman's wrists and hands, but Newman was heavier and had gotten the jump on him.

His mind roared. Darkness crept in from the edges and danced across his vision. The world faded and even the sounds of Guthrie's barks drifted away.

It ended here. In the woods. It ended without—

The pressure released, and the weight lifted from his chest.

Liam gasped and coughed. He sat up quickly, the world spinning as he threw out his arms to ward off another attack. His pulse throbbed in his ears as light rushed in to dispel the darkness.

Hot breath made him shudder. Guthrie licked his cheek and sniffed his face.

What happened?

A heavy thud shook the ground beside him and, as his gaze cleared, he looked to the right and scrambled up, fighting dizziness as he stared at Steven Newman lying face down and unconscious on the ground.

What…?

He wavered on his feet, and a strong hand gripped his elbow. "Hey, man." The words seemed to come from far away, and it took a second for his mind to grasp that he'd actually heard something. "You're going to be okay."

Blinking, he looked toward the voice. Had the deputy heard Guthrie's frantic barking? Had he left his post? He wanted to ask but his body was slow to catch up to his thoughts.

Reaching out, he grabbed the other man's arm to steady himself and met concerned blue eyes.

His own eyes widened as he scanned the man's face. Blue eyes. Dark hair. A defined jaw covered by several days' worth of beard. The face was familiar, but why? Where?

A flash of a picture raced through the pounding in his head, and his knees threatened to buckle.

He must be dead. There was no way he was still alive.

Because it was impossible that he was looking into the eyes of Kenyon Graves.

FIFTEEN

Isabella wrapped her arms around her stomach and walked to one of the floor-to-ceiling windows in Daniel Slater's house. At any other time, she'd marvel at the view, but now she could only stare blankly as she tried to hold herself together.

Several members of the DGTF had gathered at Daniel's house to wait for news. The last word they'd received was that Steven Newman wasn't at his home and that Liam and Guthrie were searching the property.

That had been nearly two hours ago.

Daniel had taken a call an hour or so ago, and he'd left the room without speaking to anyone. He hadn't returned.

Her gut screamed that something had happened to Liam. She'd seen Daniel's face when he had walked out. His jaw had been tight, and his expression had been unreadable.

Something was wrong.

Sometimes, criminals rigged their homes to explode.

Or they took up a sniper position to pick off the team one by one.

Or they—

"Hey." Lucy Lopez approached and stood beside her. Her partner, a springer spaniel named Piper, settled at her feet. "Everything's going to be okay."

Isabella had only met Lucy a couple of hours earlier. She liked the K-9 officer, who had made her laugh with stories of the therapy dogs her fiancé was training.

Isabella gave Lucy a quick smile before turning back to the window. It was a sweet sentiment, but there was no way Lucy could promise a good ending to this day.

"So, do you want to hear about the golden retriever that Micah's training?" Lucy's voice was too upbeat.

Yet, somehow, it pulled Isabella away from her fear. She turned toward the other woman. "How do you do that?"

"Do what?"

Isabella shrugged. "Distract me."

Chuckling, Lucy bent down to scratch Piper's head. "I have a lot of practice." She straightened, her expression sobering. "My daughter battles anxiety. Stories are a great way to pull her out of her thoughts. Sometimes a distraction helps her out."

"Which is why you were telling stories earlier."

"Busted." Lucy smiled. "I hope it helped."

"It did." *For a moment.* Now, the only thing that would slow her racing heart was Liam walking through the door with Guthrie, safe and sound.

"Look, Liam won't stop until he has this Newman guy in custody, but he's not obligated to report to us. We're not on this case with him."

"So what was the call that Daniel took?" It had haunted her since he'd left the room, a harbinger of doom.

A cloud flashed across Lucy's face. "I don't know." She looked out the window, clearly avoiding Isabella's gaze. "The gun trafficking case takes a lot of our resources, and Daniel's also involved in other cases for the ATF. There's no telling how many irons he has in the fire. He's also dealing with some personal issues, so that call could have been about anything."

Liam had told her briefly about Daniel's young niece suddenly appearing in his life. From what she could gather, the situation was complicated and had caused some heartache for the DGTF leader. When she could focus better, she'd have to pray for him.

Another of the team members strode across the room, a beagle at his heels. He walked with purpose, clearly carrying a message.

The K-9's name was Peanut, but she couldn't remember the officer's name. He wore a dark T-shirt and jeans, not a uniform with a nameplate, which would have been helpful.

He must have sensed her uncertainty. "West Cole. I know you've met a lot of people." He didn't wait for her to respond. Instead, he looked at Lucy. "Daniel texted. He said to hold our positions. Steven Newman is in custody, but there's more to it. Liam's here and there's something we need to see."

"Wait." Isabella's knees threatened to drop her. Her kidnapper had been arrested and Liam was alive. It was too much to take all at once. "Liam's here?" She started toward the stairs that led to the lower level of the house. She had to—

West gently grabbed her wrist, restraining her without force. "Whatever is going on, Daniel wants us to wait here."

She stopped, and West released her. What could possibly be the issue? Surely they hadn't brought Steven Newman here. She didn't want to face that man. It was too—

A sound drifted in from the hallway, and Liam appeared with Guthrie at his heels. He scanned the room until he found her. He held her gaze, then walked over to stand by the couch, his expression unreadable. He had his eyes on West Cole and Peanut.

Isabella reached for the chair beside her and gripped the

back. What was happening? She wanted nothing more than to run to him, to touch him and to reassure herself that he really was safe, but his demeanor and the heavy air of expectation in the room held her in place.

Something big was about to happen.

An unfamiliar man stepped into the room with Daniel close behind him. The man was tall and dark, with a heavy beard on his face and a look of confusion in his deep blue eyes. He looked at everyone in the room, but he didn't seem to know any of them.

"Kenyon?" West gasped, his jaw slack and his eyes wide.

Peanut yipped and raced across the room. Her barking was wild and joyful as she leaped on the stranger, pawing and jumping.

The man dropped to one knee and let the K-9 lick his face with abandon. "Hey, buddy. Hey. I... You're..." He made a downward motion with his hand.

Peanut sat obediently, though she quivered with excitement.

The man looked up at Liam. "How did I know to do that?"

"Peanut is your partner," Liam responded quietly, his hand resting on Guthrie's head.

"Peanut." The man took the K-9's face in his hands and rested his forehead against hers. "I know you, girl. I do. I don't know how or why, but I do."

West Cole hadn't moved. He continued to stare at the man as if he wasn't certain he was real.

Lucy was the first to move. She put an arm around West's waist and eased him toward the stranger, addressing Daniel as they slowly crossed the room. "Daniel? What's going on?"

Daniel dragged his hand down his face, his expression one of shock and wonder. "Clearly, Kenyon is alive. We've got a medical team coming here to evaluate him, because we don't want to take him to the hospital and risk someone seeing him. Whatever has happened to him, he doesn't remember anything, or at least not much of anything."

Kenyon dropped to sit on the floor, allowing Peanut to crawl into his lap and snuggle in as though she'd never leave. "I definitely know this girl." He looked around the room, his gaze landing on West, who had stopped several feet away. For a long moment, he said nothing as he studied the other man. "You. I might know you." He frowned, his forehead furrowing into deep lines. "I don't know what's happening." He pressed his palm to his forehead while keeping one hand on Peanut's head. "It's right on the edge, but it won't break through. I feel like…" He shook his head, agitated, and focused on the K-9 in his lap. "She makes me feel like I might know more. Who is she?"

West looked at Liam, who crouched by Kenyon. "She's your partner," he said again.

Kenyon nodded slowly. "So you were telling the truth? I'm a cop? I work with a K-9? That feels like it fits, but I don't have any memories of her. I mean, I feel like I do, but I can't see them." He looked up at West. "And you. It's like I saw you in a movie but I can't remember which one or what role you played."

West had the strangest expression on his face, as though he was both elated and defeated. "It'll come back, man. It's just…" He looked from Daniel to Liam to Lucy, who still had an arm around his waist as though she was afraid he'd collapse without support. "You're here."

"And everyone seems surprised." Kenyon looked at Liam.

West sank onto the nearest chair, and Lucy moved to stand behind him. He shook his head. "What happened? How did you get here?"

Kenyon focused on Peanut, which seemed to be the only

thing that calmed him. "I don't know. I told this guy, Liam? I told him what I know on the way over."

Liam cleared his throat. "Kenyon's memory is...scattered. He knows there are things he's forgotten, and he's been running on instinct. He's drawn to horses, so he's been working his way around ranches in the area, places he can go that don't ask a lot of questions since he has no ID and no idea who he is."

Daniel spoke for the first time. "According to Liam, Kenyon spotted someone at one of the ranches who triggered something in his memory. Turned out to be Brody Patterson—a low-level runner in the gun trafficking ring and the boyfriend of one of Steven Newman's victims."

Liam's gaze flicked to Isabella, then back to Daniel. He was holding back when she had so many questions, but finding a dead team member alive was a priority.

Daniel stared at Kenyon. "Kenyon didn't know why, but something inside drove him to keep an eye on Brody, who was arrested a few weeks back. Given that Brody had been around Newman quite a bit, that same something drew him to keep an eye on Newman as well."

"I don't know why." Kenyon looked up. "It was this thing, this instinct. I wasn't sure if I was a stalker or what I was looking for or anything. I knew I shouldn't ask them questions, but I also knew they might help me figure out what's been happening to me. Today, these guys all showed up when I was watching, and I saw a guy attack Liam and I knew I had to do something. I jumped in."

"And because of him," Liam looked around the room, "Steven Newman is in custody."

"Now here we are." Daniel looked around at his team.

"What about the kids? Have you been—" West stopped speaking when Daniel gave him a hard look. He nodded his understanding. They probably shouldn't overwhelm this man with a ton of questions. Kenyon might not even know he was a father, or it would have been the first thing out of his mouth. "Somebody needs to call Raina to let her know."

Daniel nodded. "As soon as he's been checked out by the medical team."

Liam took the opportunity while everyone was watching Kenyon to walk over to Isabella.

She finally relaxed. He was alive.

He pulled her close and lowered his chin so that his words brushed her ear. "You're safe. It's over."

She sagged against him, letting him hold her the way she should have let him hold her years ago. They had so much to talk about, but not here in front of everyone. "Liam?" She spoke into his shoulder.

"Hmm?"

She needed to feel grounded, like her world was on its feet again. She needed to be in a familiar place. Finally, the danger that had been chasing her was over. And it was because of the man standing before her, the one who had knotted up her feelings all over again. "I'm ready to go home."

It was hard to believe she was safe.

Isabella sat in Liam's SUV and stared at her front door. It was the same bright green that Aiyana had painted it a couple of years before. The landscaping hadn't changed. The house looked exactly the same.

Yet it held an air of uneasiness, fueled by the memory that someone had attacked Aiyana inside. Someone would have harmed Isabella had she been home.

She'd been hijacked, stalked, and nearly kidnapped. She'd lived in terror, looking over her shoulder. She'd witnessed the discovery of other victims and had nearly been one herself.

Slowly, Isabella pressed the button to release the seat belt. Would she ever truly feel safe again? What were Steven Newman's two kidnapping victims feeling? The ones who had been released? They'd actually been taken, held in the dark, and assaulted for days. They'd been dumped in the desert half-dead.

Did they also feel like their bodies were mired in a sickening blend of sweet relief and deep-seated survivor's guilt? Were they suffering from the red-hot fear that this wasn't over? Were they also terrified that somehow, someday they could find themselves the victim of another twisted man's game?

It had happened once. There was nothing to say that it couldn't happen again.

"Hey." Liam's fingers wrapped around hers, his voice drawing her back into the SUV. "It's going to be okay. Steven Newman is really in custody. Kenyon was able to subdue him and call for help from the deputies who were on site with my team. Newman's really going to stand trial. He really can't hurt you anymore."

"I know that, but it's hard to believe it." She offered him the best smile she could muster. "I'd really like to go inside and ... I don't know. Get a shower. Change clothes. Maybe make dinner." That might actually make her feel normal. "I think I have the stuff to make meat loaf if you'd like to have some meat loaf." She was babbling, but she didn't care. Liam knew her well enough to recognize and understand the way she dealt with overwhelming stress.

She hit the treadmill of life running at twenty miles per hour on a ten percent incline.

He chuckled. "Meat loaf sounds amazing." Shoving open the door, he moved to step out but looked over his shoulder at her. "I'll tell you what. Guthrie and I will go in with you and check the house while you wait in the living room, then you can get a shower while I give Guth a run in that big fenced back yard."

Some of the tension left her. She hadn't realized how terrified she was of walking into her own home alone. "I'd appreciate that."

"We'll check in every closet and behind every shower curtain." He winked and shut the door behind him.

Her heart swelled. He remembered.

She'd told him once, when her roommate had moved out of her apartment in college and she'd lived alone for a few weeks, that she slept better at night if she checked "in every closet and behind every shower curtain" before she went to bed. It wasn't that she thought someone was actually hiding there. It was her way of ensuring that, if she heard something go bump in the night, her imagination couldn't go into overdrive because she knew that no one was hiding in her house.

That night, and every night after until her new roommate moved in, he'd made a big show of going around the apartment before he left for the night, checking in every closet and cabinet and behind every door.

He'd been joking, but it had made her feel oddly safe as she'd shut the door behind him each night and turned the dead bolt.

Kidding or not, Liam had always been her protector.

Never more so than now.

As soon as they'd eaten a decent meal, she'd be sure they had that promised talk. They had a past to discuss... Could there be a future? These last few days, his steady presence in a time of doubt and fear had reminded her of how much she still felt for him. She'd thought she could run away from him, but she'd never stopped loving him. Now she didn't want to. She wanted him back in her life, but would he have her?

She waited for him to retrieve Guthrie from the rear of the SUV before they met at the front of the vehicle and walked toward the house together.

Everything in her wanted to pause at the door, but she pulled her key out and forced herself to keep moving. If she hesitated, the memory of Aiyana's thinly veiled fright would send her right back to Liam's SUV.

The house was cool, and the interior was dim with the curtains drawn. The minute the familiar air settled around Isabella, her spirit quieted. This was home. She was safe. The threat was over.

Liam left her in the living room and, true to his word, he and Guthrie patrolled the entire house.

When he came back downstairs, she was in the kitchen, digging through the refrigerator. "I can't make meat loaf. I don't trust the ground beef that was left in the fridge." She'd been grocery shopping several days before, when she'd expected to be home to cook instead of being terrorized by a killer. She shut the door and reached for the freezer handle. "Pretty sure I have some meatballs. Do you feel like—"

Liam walked over and shut the freezer door, then leaned one shoulder against it, watching her with eyes that said food was the last thing on his mind. "How about we talk first? I don't know that you need to cook so much as you need to rest, so I pulled up an app and ordered some burgers to be delivered in a little bit. You still like burgers, right?" His voice was low, and a slow smile played on his lips.

Guthrie sat at his feet, watching them as though understood something was about to happen.

Her heart ramping up the pace, Isabella leaned her shoulder against the freezer door as well, putting her nose to nose with Liam. "I still do." Her voice was a whisper, and she certainly hoped he understood that *she* was talking about more than her favorite food. She was talking about their future.

His breath caught.

Yeah, he understood.

And now, more than ever, she wanted that future.

His gaze roamed her face, and she let him look. She had no clue what he was searching for, but he clearly needed confirmation of something.

She gave him her most open expression, letting him discover whatever he needed.

After a long moment, he reached down, grabbed her right hand, and gently brought it up between them. He turned her palm toward him so that she was face-to-face with the ring he'd bought her almost four years earlier. The ring that had held so much promise. "I never got to ask you why you still wear it." His thumb held her palm, while his fingers wrapped around her hand.

So he'd noticed. "You have to know I didn't want to leave you. I didn't know what else to do. I was scared." She curled her fingers around his thumb, letting the ring shine between them at eye level. "I chose to leave you alive rather than have my family cause me to lose you forever." The thought of him being permanently gone from the world had been too much. She'd run in a panic, and then she'd been too afraid to come back. "I guess I always maybe kind of hoped, somewhere deep inside of me, that maybe there would come a day…" It was hard to let her secret dreams come to life.

"Come a day…what?" His voice was low, intense, gravelly.

No, that wasn't what she wanted to say. "If there wasn't you, there wasn't anybody. I didn't want to sever the connection to you. I didn't want to look for anybody else. I promised when I put that ring on that I'd be yours, and I meant it. That never changed."

Without breaking eye contact, he kissed her knuckle below the ring. "There's a lot to sort out, Izzy, but..." He lowered their hands to their sides and stepped closer, leaving no space between them. "But I know I want to sort it out. With you."

When his lips brushed hers, she forgot everything. She was home. She was safe. She was with the man she'd never stopped loving.

"Izzy?" Her name was a breath against her lips. This was—

Guthrie started whining.

With a sharp inhale, Liam dropped his forehead against hers. He was quiet until Guthrie whined again. With a frustrated exhale, he backed away from her. "I won't want to, but I have to hit Pause. That's not a call from him that I can ignore."

"I understand." She could wait. She knew his intentions, knew they had all of the time in the world to move forward.

And they *would* move forward.

"I'll let him run for a few minutes, if that's okay. But I'll definitely be back, so don't go anywhere." When she nodded, he kissed her forehead, called to Guthrie, and walked out of the back door.

He looked back twice before the door shut behind him.

Isabella turned and pressed her back against the fridge, dropping her head against the freezer door like a teenager in some romantic comedy. Yeah, he'd be back. Things would—

Someone knocked at the front door.

The burgers.

Her stomach said their delivery was right on time as she pushed away from the fridge. She glanced toward the back, where Liam had disappeared with Guthrie. She'd get the food then call them in so that Guthrie had a little bit of time to run some energy out. Then, maybe he'd rest while they…talked.

She pulled the front door open. There was a quick flash of someone standing there before something dark dropped over her head.

Before she could scream, something hard pressed into her ribs and a voice hissed, "Scream and I kill you, then I kill your boyfriend."

SIXTEEN

This was not happening.

Liam had checked every room in the small house—twice. Isabella was nowhere to be found. He'd called the DGTF and his FBI colleagues to alert them.

After loading Guthrie into the SUV, he'd floored the gas, going as fast as he dared, lights flashing, as he sped toward the FBI office in Plains City where Steven Newman was being held. It was the only place he could think to go. Maybe the man had answers.

How had Isabella disappeared?

He gripped the steering wheel tighter as he navigated past a sedan that pulled over to the shoulder to make way for him. When he'd walked into the house and found her gone, his heart had immediately dropped. His gut said she'd fled again, had been toying with him the entire time and had run off without saying goodbye.

It took a good three or four minutes for his rational mind to overcome his past heartbroken trauma. It would make no sense for Isabella to leave her own home with him in it. If she'd wanted to play runaway girlfriend, she'd have waited for a more opportune time.

No, something had happened to her.

Someone had tracked her to her home. If Steven Newman

was in custody, then who? Had her family gotten wind of Liam's return to her life? Had one of the O'Learys attacked Aiyana in the house and not Steven Newman? But how? Her father and brother were in jail, and their organization was in shambles. Surely they couldn't—

Wait. Aiyana.

The night Aiyana was attacked, she'd gone through the videos on her phone to view the external cameras at the house. There might be a clue there.

But he didn't have her number.

He was nearly to the office before he'd navigated Pennington County's phone tree and reached Aiyana.

She answered quickly. "Special Agent Barringer, is everything okay?" Given that Isabella had already told her roommate that Steven Newman was in custody, Aiyana had to know that a call from Liam meant trouble.

"Isabella is gone. I think someone took her. Is your doorbell cam active?"

Aiyana said something under her breath that he probably didn't want to interpret before she responded. "Give me a second." The phone rustled and her voice came from a distance, as though she'd turned on the speaker. "I'm checking. The notification system hasn't been working, but I can scroll back through and find— No." The word was packed with emotion. "Somebody took her. I'm sending you a screenshot. Where are you headed? I'll meet you there with a team."

"No." She couldn't. He didn't want to muddy jurisdiction. Even as his heart raced with fear, he knew he had to keep this aboveboard if they wanted to put whoever was behind this away for good. "I've got my team from the raid at Newman's house reassembling." He'd called them first thing. "We'll handle this. Sit tight."

"You know I can't do that."

"I know you have to if you don't want to jeopardize this case. We can't risk tripping on jurisdiction." Or on personal involvement. Technically, he should probably recuse himself as well, but he was in too deep, and there was no way he was backing out on Isabella now. His phone buzzed to indicate a text as he pulled into the parking lot of the nondescript office building that house the FBI field office. "I promise to keep you posted."

He hung up before Aiyana could ask more questions. It might be cruel, but if she figured out where he was headed, she could let her emotions run the show and wind up in danger.

He shoved the SUV into Park. "Lord, keep me level-headed." God was the only thing preventing him from being an emotional wreck.

He grabbed his phone from the console and swiped the screen to open Aiyana's text.

His blood ran cold.

He should have known. They all should have known.

In the screenshot, Jeralyn Locke pounded on the front door, a black hood dangling from her fingers. She held a pistol in her other hand.

They'd asked to have her brought in for questioning when Steven Newman wasn't found at home, but little effort had been put into locating her after he'd been taken into custody.

Had he dropped the ball when Kenyon Graves appeared? Was this his fault for losing focus?

Could this mistake cost Isabella her life? He'd sat feet away from the woman who had kidnapped Isabella, and he'd believed her when she said she was a victim.

Why was Jeralyn doing this?

He was halfway across the parking lot before the answer hit. He stopped in the lobby, called the chief of Meadowlark's PD, told him about Jeralyn Locke, and asked that someone be sent to her house, although the odds of her being there were slim.

He took the stairs and hurried past a sea of desks to the borrowed conference room where the team that had just disbanded was reassembling to search for Isabella.

Special Agent Camille Shay, who was working with the team interrogating Newman, met him halfway. "It's worse than we thought." She motioned for Liam to follow her up the hallway, where she opened a nondescript door and waved him inside.

On the other side of the one-way glass, Steven Newman was being interrogated. The man didn't look defeated, angry, or resigned to his fate. He almost looked relieved.

And he was talking.

Shay texted something as she closed the door behind Liam, and almost immediately, one of the agents in the interrogation room glanced at his phone, then looked at Newman. "Tell me about Jeralyn Locke."

And make it fast. The longer he stood here, the longer Jeralyn had to harm Isabella.

He was going to be sick.

He pulled in several deep, slow breaths, trying to calm his churning stomach and his racing mind. Why had he assumed this was over? Why had he left her alone in the house? Why…why…

So many *whys*.

Shay looked at him, her green eyes sympathetic. "You able to handle this?"

He nodded and turned his attention back to the interrogation. Whether he could *handle it* was beside the point. He had no choice.

Steven Newman stared at the table. "I already told you I don't want to talk about her."

"It's important."

Newman looked up, and it was as though he could see straight into Liam's eyes. "Someone back there needs to hear it? Is that what this is about? Is that why you're asking me again?" He turned his head and stared at the wall.

"No lawyer?" Liam pulled his eyes from the man in front of him to look at Shay. It was highly unusual for one not to be present.

"He doesn't want one." She shrugged. "Up until now, he's been forthcoming about everything. It almost seemed like he was glad to be caught."

Through the speakers, the other agent spoke. "Steven, you should know that Jeralyn has kidnapped a woman, and the only way to save her is for you to tell us everything, even if it's something you've already said."

It was like a switch flipped. Steven Newman's head jerked back to the interrogator, and his gaze flicked to the glass before he focused on the man across from him. His forehead creased. "Was it the artist? The one that FBI agent was with?"

Liam's breath stuttered. Had Newman been paying that much attention in the Badlands on that first evening, or had he been watching all along?

"Yes." The detective let his answer settle.

Newman stared at the mirror, seeming to consider his options.

If he didn't talk soon, it might be too late. Balling his fists, Liam leaned closer to the glass. *Come on. Talk.* Isabella needed him. He couldn't stay here forever.

But he also couldn't go out on a search with no direction. Meadowlark PD was checking Jeralyn's house, and there was still a law enforcement presence at Newman's. She wouldn't go there. The only way to know where to search was if Newman gave them a clue.

"Jeralyn didn't like what I was doing." Newman's voice suddenly punched through the speaker, lifting Liam's head. "I'd been... I'd been with women like her before. They drew me. I wanted them. For awhile, I took them and kept them and let them go. Just a couple."

Liam swallowed bile. So it was true. Newman had been assaulting women for years. He wanted to punch the wall, but he held himself in check.

Newman kept talking. "Jeralyn was different. I started following her, checking her out like usual, but she figured me out and met me head on. She wasn't like the others, so I didn't treat her like the others. Jeralyn was tough. She liked hiking and climbing, and we spent a lot of time in the Badlands. She said her dad used to take her there, but then he went away. Her mom made him go away, and she didn't like her mom. She was mean."

Did Jeralyn look like her mother? Was there some kind of strange crossover in the types of women that were kidnapped and killed?

Newman sniffed. "I didn't like what I was doing to those women, and while I was with her, that urge went away for a while, but then the urge came back. I couldn't stop. I've never been able to stop. Jeralyn helped...until it wasn't enough."

Liam dug his nails into his palms. *Talk faster.* He wanted to charge in and shake the man. *Where is Jeralyn now?*

"We'd been dating awhile, and I saw this... Well, I saw this hitchhiker. I took her, and I kept her like the others, but before I could let her go... She was out in the shed at my old place and she...she found gasoline. It was bad." He stared at his scarred hands. "That's how Jeralyn found out. She said I wasn't faithful. And that hitchhiker...she disappeared out of the shed. She was gone when I got out of the hospital. I thought maybe she got away, but now…" He ran a thumb along his wrist where, presumably, the bracelet Jeralyn had given him had once been. Likely, it was in evidence now. "She gave me a bracelet. Told me we'd been through a 'trial by fire' and we'd always be together. She moved me to a new place, helped me get a job at a ranch. I was fine until a few months ago.

"Jeralyn likes to control me, but I needed to control something." Newman dropped his gaze to the table. "I took those women, but I didn't kill them. I didn't know they were dead until it was on the news. They made Jeralyn jealous. She wanted to know why she wasn't enough for me. When she saw that two women were found, she went out to my shed and found the third one, and she took her away. She took away the next one, too."

Liam's eyes slipped shut. How had two such twisted human beings found one another? One a sadistic kidnapper, and the other a cold-blooded killer?

"Where did she take them?" The detective leaned across the table.

"I don't know." Newman sat back, his posture growing defensive. He seemed about to stop talking, but then he looked at the window again. "Out to the Badlands. She told me she let them go the way I had, but she didn't. Not if she…not if she buried one. I was going to set a trap for her, wreck her car. I went out there to stop her, but the artist came. And she was…" His face seemed to morph into something both soft and evil. "And she was perfect. And I wanted her, too."

Liam shuddered and headed for the door. He couldn't listen to this any longer. He couldn't consider the thoughts this man had directed toward Isabella.

He walked into the hall and aimed for the conference

room, pulling out his phone to call Cheyenne as he nearly ran up the hall. Maybe she could track Jeralyn or at least give them an idea of where she'd been.

Jeralyn was eliminating her "competition." And if they didn't move soon, Isabella would be next.

She had to keep her wits about herself.

Jeralyn had shoved her into the trunk, driven a few miles up the road, then bound her hands and ankles with duct tape before duct-taping her mouth. Thankfully, she'd pulled off the ski mask, or Isabella would have suffocated in the heat of the dark trunk.

She'd felt for the latch that released the trunk from the inside, but it was missing, obviously rigged to prevent escape. Had Calista Franklin and Stephanie Parry taken their last breaths in this car as well? Had they felt as much panic as she did?

Her mind screamed. Her body ached. Her heart raced.

She'd never been carsick, but she was definitely close. The darkness, the twists and turns, the heat... Although it was next to impossible, she was certain she was suffocating.

With duct tape over her mouth, she was headed for a disastrous, horrible, deadly end.

God, please. Please. Make it stop. Save me.

It would be awesome to have peace, but the terror of her situation was real. God was with her, but what was His plan? What if it wasn't the plan she wanted? What if there was no future?

Tears streamed down her heated cheeks, and she nearly choked. Would Liam think she had walked out on him again? When, and if, they found her body, it would crush him.

Nothing made sense. This had all been over...

Until it hadn't been.

Forcing herself to take measured breaths, she closed her eyes and considered her options. The only one she had was to somehow break free. She'd managed to keep her wits enough to stiffen her hands and feet as Jeralyn bound her with the duct tape. Hopefully that and sheer, terrified sweat would be enough to slip her bonds. With measured movements, she twisted her wrists and ankles, then pulled them apart as far as she could, over and over again.

There was very little room to maneuver, and she couldn't sit up, but she had enough space to move her hands and feet.

It was tough to tell if her hard work was having any effect, but it gave her something to focus on besides panic. The tape cut into her wrists, chafing and burning, but maybe, it seemed a little looser with every twist.

She bounced as the car slowed and bumped along a road that crunched beneath the tires.

They were somewhere in the Badlands, there was no doubt. The increasing heat, the feeling of the vehicle as it rolled forward, and the lack of sound from outside all pointed to the inevitable.

Perhaps there really was a "killing field" in the Badlands. The way Jeralyn was behaving said that, if she wasn't the killer, then she was a willing accomplice.

The car slowed until it was coasting, as though Jeralyn was searching for something.

Probably the best place to bury her body.

Isabella shuddered and choked then started working faster at her bonds. She couldn't stop now. She couldn't give in to fear.

Time was running out.

Sweat ran down her face to mingle with her tears. The inside of the trunk was a dark oven.

And still she worked.

As Jeralyn rolled on, Isabella stopped to reevaluate. She may not get her hands free in time, but there was enough movement in her fingers to unwrap her ankles.

Twisting as slowly as she could to avoid making noise that might tip off Jeralyn, Isabella felt around her ankles until she found the ends of the duct tape. She worked as quickly as she could to unwrap the bonds.

When her ankles were free, she sank to the floor in relief, the sand and dirt in the carpet grinding into her cheek.

If nothing else, she could run.

She allowed herself a minute to regroup. Maybe, if she shoved her foot between her hands, there would be enough force to—

The car rolled to a stop, and the engine died.

She was out of time.

With duct tape still binding her wrists, Isabella crouched as well as she could in the tight space and waited.

And waited.

Nearby, a sound broke the silence.

An engine fired up, something smaller than a car, then roared away into the distance.

Isabella ripped the duct tape from her mouth and bit back a scream. She braced herself against the back of the car and pushed against the rear seats, but nothing moved. They were too heavy. Something was braced against them.

There was no way out.

Panic overtook her. She shook. Screamed. Cried out.

It was hot. Stifling. The air was too thin.

Isabella breathed faster and faster, gulping air until spots swirled in the darkness of the trunk.

Jeralyn Locke had left her in the broiling wilderness to bake.

SEVENTEEN

"Cheyenne, tell me you have something for me." Liam prayed with everything in him that she did. If Cheyenne was lost, then all was lost.

Liam was heading up a line of law enforcement vehicles headed to the Badlands in search of Isabella and Jeralyn. There was no way Jeralyn would go to where she had buried the other women, not knowing that law enforcement had already located them. No, she would find another place, somewhere off the beaten path. Since they'd been unable to locate any real estate records in her name or in Steven Newman's, their best assumption was that she'd headed for the wilds.

Given that the Badlands were nearly four hundred square miles of "off the beaten path," she could have taken Isabella anywhere...

If their educated guess was even correct. They could be in the Black Hills, in the—

"I've managed to see where Jeralyn's vehicle has been before, though I'm not able so far to get real-time data from her GPS. I'm working on getting emergency authorization to access her phone so we can track her that way." Cheyenne's voice came through the speakers in Liam's SUV, somehow both reassuring and terrifying.

Please, God, don't let us be too late. Jeralyn had over an hour on them, and their only hope was that Cheyenne could use GPS data to locate them, hopefully before the worst could happen.

He could not find Isabella only to lose her again.

In the rear of the SUV, Guthrie had planted his feet and stood with his nose to the wire caging that separated him from Liam. He whimpered softly, picking up on the tension in the vehicle and in their voices.

He reached up and placed his hand against the screen, letting Guthrie lick his fingers. The K-9 settled down after the reassurance, curling up with his back against the door.

"Liam?" Cheyenne sounded urgent. "Talk to me."

"I'm here. Does anything ping on the historical data for her vehicle?" That was the logical first place to start.

There was the sound of tapping through the speakers as Cheyenne worked her tech awesomeness. "Jeralyn has made several trips out to the Badlands. Her car's GPS history places her at the burial sites at around the time the bodies would have been left there. It also places her at a site about two miles from that camping area, deeper in the Badlands where there's more shelter on those same days, about an hour before she likely placed the remains."

Liam swallowed a knot in his throat. There was no need for Cheyenne to say more. That was likely the spot where she'd ended the lives of Stephanie Parry and Calista Franklin.

"I'm sending you the location."

His SUV's screen lit, and he pushed the button to download the directions. The team behind him would follow his lead.

The directions appeared.

Twenty minutes away.

So much could happen in twenty minutes.

He tightened the muscles in his leg to keep from pressing the accelerator to the floor. Spinning out in a fiery crash wouldn't help anybody. "Is she there now?"

"I'm working on it."

It felt like the silence stretched forever. How could she have old data and not current? How could—

"Got it. The car is near that location, and it's stopped. It's been stopped for about fifteen minutes."

Too much time. Jeralyn had strangled both Calista Franklin and Stephanie Parry. It was the kind of death that was personal and spoke of her sick jealousy. She saw Newman's victims as rivals, as standing in the way of her relationship with a horrible man. Putting her hands around their necks meant she could look them in the eye. She could watch as she put to death her perceived competition.

Was she doing the same to Isabella, even now?

Inhaling sharply, Liam pressed the accelerator down. "Is there a faster route?"

"No. And, Liam? I can see your speed through your GPS. Check yourself. You've got half a dozen people on your tail. You don't want to be responsible for someone getting hurt, and you don't want someone deciding you're a liability and pulling you off of this."

He lifted his foot slightly. She was right in more ways than one. "I should have let someone else handle this."

"Probably." The answer was blunt and true. "It's too late now, so you have to be rational. I'm right here on the line to help you do that. Okay?"

He nodded, gratitude easing some of his tension. Where would he be without the Dakota Gun Task Force? He'd had amazing people around him in the FBI, but he'd never been a member of a family like this one. "Thanks." It was tough to force the word out.

"No problem. We're all here for you."

Some of them literally were. Two cars back, Daniel and Jenna were keeping pace, heading out to rescue the woman he loved.

Until he reached Isabella's location, he needed to focus on something else. "Know what doesn't make sense to me?"

"Why did Jeralyn give Steven Newman up to you guys?"

That wasn't it. "No, that makes sense to me. She panicked and covered her own rear on that one. She probably thought she could warn him and get him out before we showed up and that they could meet up somewhere down the road when things cooled down. It's something else that bothers me."

"Let me guess." Cheyenne's voice was both serious and light, as though she was trying to calm a half-wild dog. "You're wondering why Jeralyn buried one victim but left the other ritualistically posed?"

His team understood him. "It doesn't make sense."

"Posing Calista Franklin to face the sun made it look like something different was happening. Remember, Newman was releasing the women. Jeralyn was killing them. She had to find a way to throw investigators off their trail. She likely wanted to make it look like a ritualistic serial killer was involved. Then again, there's a simpler explanation."

"Like?" Following this rabbit trail helped his mind to stop spinning horrible images.

"Digging in the Badlands is hard work. Maybe it was efficiency. After all, Jeralyn Locke isn't too smart. She drove her own car out to the crime scene. She had to know we could track GPS. Eventually, we'd…" She trailed off.

His heart hit double time as adrenaline shocked his system. "What?"

"Okay, listen to me, Liam. I've got new intel, but I'm not sure what it means."

He steeled himself for the worst. If only life were like the movies, where they could reposition a satellite to see what was happening. "I'm ready." He wasn't, but he had no choice.

"The car is not moving, but Jeralyn's phone is heading away from the vehicle across some pretty desolate country at a decent rate of speed."

"All-terrain vehicle?" This all screamed of a predetermined plan. "If she's had one staged all along, then that might explain how Steven Newman got away so quickly when he attacked Isabella the first time."

"I'll work on getting a helicopter up to track her while you work on getting to the car. Just hang tight. We're all praying. I'll be in touch."

He nodded, but his mouth was too dry to speak as Cheyenne ended the call.

If Jeralyn Locke had left the car behind, then chances were she'd already finished what she'd started.

No. He couldn't think like that. If he did, he'd slam the brakes and never move again.

About a mile from his destination, Liam forced himself to pull over and wait for his team to gather. They pulled off to the side and circled up on the gravel road that led to a secluded overlook. From the looks of the road, it was rarely used, although the dust had been recently disturbed.

He met the eyes of the half dozen men and women around him, his mind struggling to form words.

The truth was clear.

He couldn't lead this team.

His hands shook, and his heart rate was too high. If something happened that demanded he respond quickly, his emotions had already compromised his reasoning.

He looked at Daniel. "Can you take point?"

When Daniel nodded, Liam quickly briefed the team he'd

worked with at Steven Newman's house on who Daniel was, then he gave them the intel that Cheyenne had provided.

Daniel was a tactically minded ATF agent, and he quickly laid down a plan for them to approach the vehicle. Liam would wait by his SUV until they cleared the area, then he would be allowed in.

He didn't want to consider why Daniel had him stay behind, what his task force leader and friend might be protecting him from.

They rolled forward until they were around the bend from the vehicle, then exited silently. The team moved forward quietly, weapons drawn, while Liam waited by his vehicle.

They rounded a rock formation rapidly with multiple shouts identifying themselves as law enforcement.

Liam's heart raced. His palms were slicked with sweat. His prayers were unintelligible.

"Clear!" Daniel's voice seemed to come from a distance, barely audible through the pounding in Liam's ears.

He raced around the rock.

A dark blue sedan sat close to the rock, broiling in the sun. In what seemed to be slow motion, one of the deputies broke the front window, then reached in and popped the trunk.

He couldn't wait any longer. The world seemed small, narrow, focused on the trunk. It felt as though he was underwater. Muffled sound. Lagging movements.

The team parted as he reached the vehicle.

Isabella lay in the trunk, as still as death. Her skin was red. Her face was damp. Her eyes were closed.

Heedless of protocol, he reached for her, panic surging as he felt the heat of her skin.

But...

But she was breathing.

As he touched her, she gasped. Her eyes fluttered open, her gaze landing on him with confusion and panic.

He didn't look away from her as sound and light rushed back into his world. "Get a helicopter. We need to get her out of here and we need to get her cooled off. Fast."

He lifted her from the vehicle and rushed her to his SUV. Someone opened the front door and he sat her inside, taking a bottle of water that was passed to him. Mechanically, he held it to her lips.

She was safe. She was alive.

But she wasn't out of the woods.

If she never flew in a helicopter again, it would be too soon. If she never saw the inside of a hospital again, it would be too soon.

If she ever had to leave her house again, it might be too soon.

She waved off Aiyana's offer to help as they walked into the house after her discharge from a one-night stay in the hospital and made her way to the couch, feeling off-balance and woozy.

It was either some raging PTSD or the effects of dehydration after nearly cooking in the trunk of Jeralyn Locke's car. Although the nurses had pumped her full of saline, she still felt as parched as the Badlands themselves.

Aiyana watched her carefully. "You need anything? Water? Food?"

"For you to not hover?" She settled onto the couch and let her head fall onto the cushions. The release of being home washed over her, and with it came a wave of guilt. "I'm sorry. You're just trying to help."

"And you're battling trauma. It's okay." Her roommate crossed the den. "I'm going to clear the house just to be sure, then I'll make some lunch." She disappeared up the stairs, and her footfalls came through the ceiling as she moved from room to room.

Isabella closed her eyes, but she couldn't relax. A deputy sat outside of their house. Aiyana was on guard duty inside.

Jeralyn Locke was still out there somewhere.

And Liam was searching for her.

Pursing her lips, she exhaled slowly. *God, I'm trusting You with all of this.*

If she didn't, she'd lose her mind.

She gave up on relaxing and picked her e-reader up off of the coffee table, scrolling through titles until she found what she was looking for.

Two pages in, she dropped the device onto the couch and stood.

Pacing to the window, she stared into her back yard. On a normal Saturday, she'd be working in the flower beds or finishing up the paint on the thrift store patio furniture she'd bought a few weeks earlier.

This wasn't a normal Saturday. Thanks to her time in Jeralyn's trunk, she was heat-sensitive and couldn't be out of the air conditioning for long. She'd only spent one night in the hospital on IV fluids and being cooled down, but the doctors had cautioned her to slowly work her way back into a routine.

Her whole life was up in the air. Worst of all, her relationship with Liam had no definition.

They hadn't had the opportunity to talk once. He'd stayed physically close at the hospital but had kept his emotional distance. Maybe he was giving her space. Maybe he'd changed his mind.

She twisted the sapphire ring on her right hand. She loved him, that much she knew. But did they have a future? Could they, with Jeralyn Locke still hanging over her life?

Aiyana's voice drifted down from upstairs, but it was impossible to make out the words. Likely, she was updating someone on their situation at the house.

She was so tired of being a *situation*.

Isabella walked to the couch and picked up her e-reader again. She opened the book, but she didn't bother reading a word.

Aiyana came down the stairs, flopped beside her and took the device from her hands. "You're in your feelings pretty deep if you're reading *A Tree Grows in Brooklyn*. All of the sads in that one."

"And all of the hope." While the main character's life had been marred by poverty and tragedy, she'd always risen above with imagination and hope. "I could use some of that right now."

Passing the book back to her, Aiyana propped her feet on the coffee table. She picked at a hangnail, focused on her thumb. "Want to talk?"

"I want my life back." Actually, it was so much more than that. "I want a lot of things."

"Things like Liam?" Aiyana dropped her hands to her lap. Picking her phone up from the coffee table, Aiyana glanced at it, then stood. "I'm going to get a snack and eat my feelings. You want anything?" She didn't wait for an answer. As she walked past the front door, she reached over and popped the lock before disappearing into the kitchen.

Isabella jumped up. What was Aiyana thinking, unlocking the front—

Liam stepped in with Guthrie behind him.

At the sight of him, Isabella sank onto the couch, her knees weak. He was here. What did that mean?

Shutting the door behind him, Liam carefully locked the dead bolt. He'd confessed to her at the hospital that he felt guilty for leaving her in a position to be taken by Jeralyn Locke.

Liam commanded Guthrie to take a spot near the door, then walked over and sat down on the coffee table, his knees touching hers. "Hey."

Something in his gaze was off, almost as though he was hiding something.

Or as though he had something to say that he didn't want to say.

She dropped her gaze to his knees. He hadn't come back for her. He was here to say goodbye. To say this wouldn't work. To say he couldn't trust her.

And she couldn't blame him.

"Hey." He repeated his greeting, then tipped her chin up to look at him.

She could get lost in those hazel eyes. It might be a cliché, but it was true. She'd once thought she could stare into them forever, and that hadn't changed.

Right now, those eyes were soft, sympathetic...and they were drinking her in as though he thought he might never see her again.

She dared to reach over with her right hand and smooth down his wild hair, which looked like he'd run his hands through it more than once. He looked as tired as she felt.

Liam captured her hand and held it between them, planting a kiss on her knuckle.

Hope.

Did she dare trust the feeling?

Lowering their joined hands, he ran his thumb along her knuckles, sending the most incredible shivers up her arm. He stared at their fingers before he looked up at her again. "It's over. Jeralyn Locke is in custody."

"Wait. What?" Had she heard him right? She withdrew

her hand, the unexpected shock. The words wouldn't sink in. It was over. She was safe.

They were safe.

Isabella grabbed her knees and held on. "What happened?"

"She was desperate when she came after you, unhinged knowing that she'd gotten Steven Newman arrested. She made mistake after mistake, not the first of which was leaving you in her own car."

Isabella swallowed hard, trying to beat down the memory of her desperation in that trunk.

Liam gently took her hand. "She left herself with nowhere to go, no way to run. We caught up to her at Steven Newman's house, where she was trying to take his truck to make her escape. She's being questioned now. You're safe."

"Because of you."

"Well, me and a few other people." He turned her hand over and ran his finger down her palm. "You have to know I will do everything in my power, for the rest of my life, to protect you from people like her."

The best kind of shiver ran up her arm at his touch. Was he saying—

He leaned closer, his voice dropping low as a smile teased his lips.

Lips she couldn't stop looking at.

His voice dropped to a whisper. "I mean that literally. *The rest of my life*, because I love you, Isabella Katherine Whitmore." His gaze dipped to her lips then back to her eyes. Slowly, he leaned forward and brushed her lips with his. He pulled her close, deepening the kiss.

Just when she thought she'd lose all of her breath, he eased away and dropped his head to her shoulder. "I know I said that we needed to talk, but do we? I don't need to discuss what I already know. What I need..." He lifted her hand, the sapphire he'd slipped onto her finger four years earlier sparkling between them. "What I need is for this—" he tapped the ring, then picked up her left hand "—to go back on this hand." He pressed a kiss to her left ring finger, then backed away to look at her. "If that's what you want."

It was very much what she wanted. She didn't need to talk either. She'd never stopped loving him. Had spent too long away from him. She was ready to start right now, living the rest of their lives together.

Without a word, she held out both hands, palms down and fingers straight, daring him to make the move.

Without tearing his gaze from hers, he slipped the ring from her right hand to her left.

As it slid up her finger, he kissed her again...

And she promised to stay by his side forever.

EPILOGUE

"Daddy! Look at me!" One of Kenyon's twin sons jumped off of a low stump in Daniel's back yard.

Isabella had only met the boys this morning, so she was still unsure which was Beacon and which was Austin. One thing was sure...they were their father's children.

Kenyon sat in one of the chairs that had been pulled up in a circle near where the kids chased one another. He smiled and shouted encouragement to his sons, but his expression was guarded. It was clear his memory was still filled with holes and that, while something in him recognized his children and he was putting on a good act, he still had a long way to go.

The only person missing from the circle was Jenna Morrow. The DGTF had a thin lead in Cold River, a small town a couple of hours from Fargo, North Dakota, and she'd gone to check it out. When it came to the gun trafficking ring, the task force left no stone unturned.

Liam picked up her hand and laced his fingers through hers, resting their joined hands on the arm of his chair. He leaned across the gap toward her. "No frowns today. This is a good day."

She smiled and sat back in the chair, determined to relax.

Her tormentors were in custody. They couldn't harm her or anyone else again.

Liam was right. It was a good day. They'd announced their engagement to the DGTF and had received a rousing round of applause. She'd even received congratulations from some familiar faces. She hadn't realized that Deputy Zach Kelcey was on the task force. She'd interviewed his wife, Eden, and had drawn a sketch for them a couple of months before. They'd greeted her like old friends.

This group truly was a family, one she was glad to be joining.

Even the children all acted like they were cousins. Kenyon's twins were running the show, although they were only three. Daniel's niece, Joy, toddled from adult to adult, handing out hugs and delighting in the attention.

Lucy's young daughter, Annalise, stuck close to her mother and Micah Landon, playing quietly with her little Yorkshire terrier. Though she watched the roughhousing of the other children with interest and a smile, she seemed content to observe.

This impromptu meetup had been born out of the team's desire to see Kenyon for themselves. He'd spent a couple of days in the hospital under observation, and his visitors had been limited. Many of the task force members were openly watching him, shocked he was alive and likely wondering if he would recover his memory. He was to begin working with a memory specialist the next day. The doctors were positive, but they cautioned it might take time.

Isabella kept most of her attention on Raina McCord, Kenyon's best friend and the woman who had been raising his children in his absence. She kept a close eye on him, and there was something about her expression that—

"So..." Liam squeezed her hand and drew her out of her thoughts. "You doing okay with this big crowd of people?"

She squeezed his fingers in return and nodded. This little get-together at Daniel's marked the first time she'd been out of the house in days, but she was doing fine. "Even better because you're here."

He winced. "When did you get so sappy, woman?" His smile softened the words, then he looked around the circle at his friends. "We're going to be okay."

"Yes, we are." More than okay. Because they'd found one another. Now she knew what it meant to be safe with Jesus and with the man He had placed in her life to love.

Now she knew that she could truly live without fear... and in love.

* * * * *

*If you enjoyed Liam's story, don't miss Jenna's story next!
Check out* Threat of Revenge
and the rest of the Dakota K-9 Unit series!

Chasing a Kidnapper
by Laura Scott, April 2025

Deadly Badlands Pursuit
by Sharee Stover, May 2025

Standing Watch
by Terri Reed, June 2025

Cold Case Peril
by Maggie K. Black, July 2025

Tracing Killer Evidence
by Jodie Bailey, August 2025

Threat of Revenge
by Jessica R. Patch, September 2025

Double Protection Duty
by Sharon Dunn, October 2025

Final Showdown
by Valerie Hansen, November 2025

Christmas K-9 Patrol
by Lynette Eason and Lenora Worth, December 2025

*Available only from Love Inspired Suspense
Discover more at LoveInspired.com*

Dear Reader,

I hope you are enjoying reading about the Dakota Gun Task Force! It is always fun to get to work with other writers, especially writers as awesome as these ladies! They are a talented group, and it's always an honor to work with them.

As I was writing Isabella and Liam's story, it struck me that Liam had a lot to forgive. Isabella had deeply wounded him, and he was still suffering three years later. Forgiveness can be difficult. In Liam's case, it was made a bit easier because he learned that he didn't know the whole story.

God knows our whole story. If you've been around awhile, you know I love Psalm 139. God knows our every thought, word and action from beginning to end. You could say He knows "the good, the bad and the ugly." The beautiful part of that is how much He loves us in spite of it all. "Good, bad or ugly," His love doesn't change. Out of that love, He sent Jesus to take on our punishment on the cross so that we could be forgiven and restored to Him. And that, dear reader, is truly "the whole story." I pray it is part of your story. If it's not, reach out to me or to any of the ladies of the DGTF series. We'd love to pray for you.

Thank you for spending time with us all. Your time spent reading is a gift to us, and we appreciate it. Enjoy the rest of the series!

Jodie

Harlequin Reader Service

Enjoyed your book?

Try the perfect subscription for Romance readers and get more great books like this delivered right to your door.

See why over 10+ million readers have tried Harlequin Reader Service.

Start with a Free Welcome Collection with free books and a gift—valued over $20.

Choose any series in print or ebook.
See website for details and order today:

TryReaderService.com/subscriptions